WORDS ARE SOMETHING ELSE

Writings from an Unbound Europe

DAVID ALBAHARI

WORDS ARE SOMETHING ELSE

Translated by Ellen Elias-Bursać

Edited and with an Afterword by Tomislav Longinović

Foreword by Charles Simić

NORTHWESTERN UNIVERSITY PRESS

EVANSTON, ILLINOIS

Northwestern University Press
Evanston, Illinois 60208-4210

Printed in the United States of America

ISBN 0-8101-1305-8 (CLOTH)
ISBN 0-8101-1306-6 (PAPER)

Library of Congress Cataloging-in-Publication Data

Albahari, David, 1948–
[Short stories. English. Selections]
Words are something else / David Albahari ; translated by Ellen Elias-Bursać ; edited and with an afterword by Tomislav Longinović ; foreword by Charles Simić.
p. cm. — (Writings from an unbound Europe)
ISBN 0-8101-1305-8 (cloth : alk. paper). — ISBN 0-8101-1306-6 (paper : alk. paper).
1. Albahari, David, 1948– —Translations into English. I. Elias-Bursać, Ellen. II. Title. III. Series.
PG1419.1.L335A24 1996
891.8'235—dc20 96-12339
CIP

The paper used in this publication meets the minimum requirements of the American National Standard for Information Sciences—Permanence of Paper for Printed Library Materials, ANSI Z39.48-1984

CONTENTS

PART III

■ □ ■ □ ■

FOREWORD

Charles Simić

It seems that we learn something about art when we experience what the word solitude is meant to designate.

Maurice Blanchot

THE CLAIM OFTEN MADE BY WESTERN INTELLECTUALS THAT THE worst political systems produce the best literature is nothing more than wishful thinking. Eastern Europe and Russia have had great writers, but they were and continue to be solitary heroic figures and an exception to the rule. The great majority of writers do what is safe and expected of them. They peddle the official version of reality with more or less skill, and a few of them even with a touch of genius. That's what the opportunists do everywhere in order to avoid becoming outcasts. A writer or a poet in Eastern Europe who refuses the temptations of ideological or ethnic identification is reserving for himself the role of a pariah. If that writer is Jewish, as Albahari is, then he can expect even more trouble. The individual wary of the latest groupthink has no defenders. Marx had no use for him, nor do the nationalists today. What every collectivist program demands is the cult of the great leader and the obedient, cheering masses shouting, as they used to do in Mao's day, "the world is progressing, and the future is bright." If someone nevertheless chooses to stand in the corner with his back to the crowd, he should expect to be stoned sooner or later.

The stubborn individual who lives the life of an exile in his own community is Albahari's hero. His strange behavior, his gloom and sense of forbidding as if he were living next door to a prison camp or a place of execution, is his subject. The historical context, rarely alluded to in Albahari's stories, must not be forgotten. We are not in North Dakota or Switzerland. The past horrors and those still to come cast their shadow on the protagonists of these stories. When the Balkan orphan factories are working around the clock, the nature of reality and the reality of writing itself become serious questions, as they never do for the so-called realist writers who take their cue from official ideology. As Albahari well knows, the awareness of the fate of the individual makes the existence of "objective history" impossible and literature difficult to write.

The novel is undoubtedly the richest literary form yet devised for understanding the variety of human experiences, but it usually has bigger fish to fry. There's an incongruity between its linear plot and its large vision of society and the minute experience of the solitary self. The lyric poet writes about those rare moments when time stops. The short stories Albahari writes are like poems in that respect. They have touched upon something essential, something difficult to put into words, and so they circle back on themselves. It's not the plot that sticks in our minds after reading him, but certain images, so haunting and powerful they could have come out of our own dreams. His stories are like collages, pieces of a much larger puzzle—perhaps not even the same puzzle—brought together in an attempt to fit them together. As he reminds us in one of them, "Beauty is in presentiment, in hints, in expectation of the whole." It is not surprising, therefore, that his stories are mostly a few pages long.

The cast of characters often recurs from story to story.

Typically, there's a father and a mother, both aged, a son who is a writer, a sister who gets married and moves away, and eventually a wife. The family is Jewish, the place is Communist Yugoslavia, a country where most Jews perished in the Second World War. They live quiet, nearly anonymous lives in a small apartment in a town on the river Danube across from the city of Belgrade. They do not have many visitors. Among the few who come are Godzilla the Sea Monster, The Man Who Shot Liberty Valance, and Antonio das Mortes, the Brazilian bandit from the movie of the same name. The family members are nearly inseparable, and yet each one is as solitary and as inscrutable to the others as if he were Melville's Bartleby.

The secretiveness of every family has its moments of mythical resonance. The heart of Albahari's poetics is that gray area between myth and reality where every blurred image and haphazard incident may contain the answer to the mystery of our identity. "We are never real historians, but always poets, and our emotion is perhaps nothing but an expression of the poetry that is lost," says the French philosopher Gaston Bachelard. The childhood world and the family life we remember is an interior universe full of lost clues and tantalizing hints. Like any great writer, Albahari makes his most intimate reveries our own.

"Memories are, of course, tricky, even though they are all we have to feel that we truly exist," Albahari writes. For such memory, often on the very limits of memory, interiors with their inanimate objects as the mature witnesses to everything said or left unsaid, have as much weight as people who were present that day. How we remember, talk about, mourn, and construct stories out of such fragments is what he is interested in. One lies to tell the truth, of course. However, the knowledge that only imagination can recover the flavor of old reality is not an easy knowledge—and so one writes. Only rarely have the full literary and philosophical implications of what it means to be a writer at the end of a long and vile century been articulated as well as in these stories.

If not for translation, we would have to depend on CNN for our knowledge of the rest of the world. The true multiculturalists have always been the little-appreciated translators without whom we would be condemned to a self-satisfied literary and intellectual provincialism. With this collection of stories, so ably translated by Ellen Elias-Bursać, Albahari, who has already been widely translated in Europe, makes his first appearance in English. He belongs to that select group of writers in the world today whose work may be said to be indispensable.

PART I

■ □ ■ □ ■

THREE BUS STOPS HOME

THERE WERE DAYS WHEN FATHER AND I WENT OFF TO WALK along the river, and further: along the dilapidated, uncertain steps through the Jewish graveyard to Muhar, and slowly, along the main street, home. We were the same height then, and I wore his summertime, olive-green jacket, tailored ten years earlier in Italy: in 1952. We didn't talk. We moved through the dense shadows and the even denser shadows; we inhaled, with a gentle trembling of nostrils, the smell of the Danube; we draped ourselves in it like a fisherman's wife in her kerchiefs; only the sound of the oars, the restless buzz of a motor, and, on the other shore, equally still, a massive, intractable wall of trees, a city of girls bent over their mirrors. The walk didn't last long: precisely as long as it took to traverse those points, without dialogue, without stopping—two or three times we'd stop at crosswalks and up by the cemetery—in a charge through the empty pathways, down the endless steps (not the first ones, behind Radecki, but the others, the cemetery steps, much sturdier) to Muhar, where, if it started to rain, we'd catch a bus—three stops home.

I didn't intend to, but sometimes I really wanted to stop him, to ask: "What do you think, how long can this last? How many more times will we be able to walk like this, wordless, silent? Can we? Do we?" Then I still wasn't sure I'd get taller than him, though I thought I might. At night I often dreamed of flying; in the morning I was thrilled when my trouser legs were shorter, my shoes pinched. We walked together, the same height, the same shoulders, his stomach only hinting at corpulence, though even now he isn't fat: his skinny, stringy limbs the very opposite of corpulence, the steep bulge under his belt. Infectious jaundice had left tangible traces on him—I don't know what—but when he'd turn or look, mid-stride, twisted, over his shoulder, you could say: this man has been to the end and he's on his way back. Then we lived in Ć., a prominent doctor's family, in regular attendance at the movie theaters, residents of a prewar villa with a massive oak door above which someone had scribbled, among the many swallows' nests, a large red five-pointed star. Afterward, when he got better, my mother was left with the legacy of making fresh cheese, as prescribed by his diet, and he began to work, at first on a shorter schedule, then a full week, never quite making it to head of his department (if you don't count his position as director in Peć, in Kosovo immediately after the war—the sole physician in the only gynecological clinic in the entire region) in Ć., or in Zemun.

There were days when I didn't feel like going, but I started getting dressed as soon as he took off his slippers in the kitchen. By then he had stopped using the switch as an educational method, he no longer summoned me into the bathroom except in the most remarkable circumstances, but even when I was outside in the yard I would come in, change shoes, wash my hands and face, leaving black smudges on the towel when I dried off. He was ready, pristine in his one summer suit (he had only a single pair of trousers in Peć, and an adjusted suit jacket; Mother would get up before he did to dry them a bit more with the iron) and a carefully knotted tie. Sometimes he tidied the hastily and clumsily arranged part in my hair, and then mute, unaccustomed to talk, he'd be ready to retreat abruptly. We set out together—he and Mother exchanging kisses, she and I grins—right into the bright light of day, through the oval park, through the old lumberyard, to the shore of the river. Now there is no park.

"Civilization devoured it," Mother says, leaning on the windowsill. And the trolley bus stop has been moved. In general: we have lost that important, central position, but we haven't budged; it's the town that's been moving around us.

On the river, fishermen and their wives were wrapped in kerchiefs of bright colors; in front of Radecki, we came across the occasional late swimmer. We climbed up, high, to the cemetery gates. We stopped to rest. Father took a soft folded rag from his pocket and wiped the dust from his shoes.

If we decided to take the steps by the Tower, first we'd survey everything—the Danube, the city, the plains—and then we'd arrive at the slow-moving main street. From there we'd move straight on through two streets and two squares, home. At first we lived in a small room, which was also a passageway, on October 22nd Street. We arrived in that room from the seven-room villa in Ć. one December and found Father already ensconced (one bed, one armchair). We stayed there long enough for me to have my childhood and my first sins. Later we moved to Lenin Street, staying with chance acquaintances, half-Jewish like us (if we count Mother's conversion in 1936, when she changed from the Orthodox to the Jewish faith), half-affluent as we were. Then to Dubrovnik Street, at my aunt's, still in Zemun—I was still a virgin, fearful of natural drives, anxious about the murky river. Then we moved here, to Karageorge Square, and here we've stayed. When we chose a different route, along a number of house lots, we'd come to a long staircase, wide and harder to climb, and we'd separate, each leaning on his own railing—the same, distant, parallel blood.

. . .

On my way back from the drugstore, I stopped by the store window of a little tobacco shop. I held my breath. An entire treasure trove lay before me: balloons, a shiny white ambulance, green jeeps, mysterious packages marked TROJAN. And when someone touched me on the shoulder, asking, "Whom do you belong to, young man?" I turned away without looking. Then I looked up and saw them: Father and Mother, the only flesh I knew at that time (as a ten-year-old), and I said: "You," unaware that I was realizing this for the first time.

"Both of you," I added.

. . .

As I said: whenever it started raining, because summer was on the wane, it would get gloomy over New Belgrade, and we'd catch the bus—three bus stops home.

■ □ ■ □ ■

IS THIS AGE, KID?

"MOTHER," I SAID, AND MOVED TO TOUCH HER FACE. IF I touched her, I thought, I'd feel new wrinkles or the tiredness in the big bags under her eyes. I made do with the pain residing in her face and didn't touch her.

"Listen, kid," said the woman behind me, "she's sleeping right now. Why don't you take a walk and come back later? Then she'll be up and ready to talk."

I turned. She was leaning on her elbow and her breasts were tumbling out of the unbuttoned nightgown right among the long strands of hair, almost down to her listless fingers.

"Pardon?" I said.

"I said," said the woman, pushing her hair back, "take a little walk. Come back when she wakes up."

"How can I . . . " I said, "you know she's my mother."

"Nonsense," she said, "I've got a mother, too. Everyone has a mother." She looked around the room: the other women were sleeping or looking out the window. "But we don't go waking them up when they're fast asleep."

"Do you know . . . ," I said.

"Who can imagine," said the woman, "what she is dreaming right now. Who knows," she said, eyes closed, "where she is. There are so many lovely meadows, streams, elms, birds in nests." Then she fell silent. I thought she'd dozed off, but she opened her eyes slowly, the eyelids opened a crack.

"What is your name?" she asked.

"Mother," I said again, but she couldn't wake up. No one would wake up to such a soft voice. "Would you . . . ," I looked at the woman's face, "tell her I was here?"

She said nothing, a smile seemed to slide over her features.

"Please," I said. "Please."

"A person comes to happiness by different routes," my father said. "Mine," he'd stop and measure the other shore with a glance, "is always to go straight ahead. If a man sets his mind to it," he turned his face to me, "there are no obstacles. In front of him is the path and he walks. If he is determined, he'll get to the end—if he isn't, there are many other paths leading into brambles."

"And he'll take them?" I asked needlessly, and by the way he raised his eyebrows I could guess the answer in advance.

"He will," confirmed my father.

My sister regularly avoided conversations, or she'd retire, in the heat of a discussion, to bed. Her skin was pale, very pale, like the finest marble, but her features have never changed. I have no need to leaf through old picture albums: memory suffices. From the day I first saw her, when I understood that the face smiling over me was hers, that hers were that long, narrow nose, the compressed lip, the small, dark eyes, my sister hasn't changed—not a single part of her face has gotten bigger or more prominent, everything is just as I remember it, as I know it, as I recognize it. Then her hips got bigger. They spread, and Mother smoothed them because they resembled hers. That was when I first heard Father talk about genes and hereditary traits, but Mother didn't care.

"The hips are mine," she said. "And the thighs are mine. And the waist."

Everything else, however, was different. Mother walked bent over, as if contorted with pain, constantly hurrying, while my sister walked straight and tense, like a soldier with a calm face, which was, of course, a front. Mother was careful about the order of things; my sister was not. "Youth," you might have said at the start, but it lasted, abandoned in the form of forgotten dresses and discarded stockings, volumes scattered messily on the table.

"You'll get married," my mother would say, "you'll see." Father refrained from comment. He kept quiet during dinner, he kept quiet after his shift at the hospital, he kept quiet in the early evening, before bed.

"Is that age?" I wondered. (At this point I was fascinated with age.)

Father, I say, kept quiet, or he'd go off, alone, pretty far from home.

"Please," I repeated. It seemed to me that what I wanted to say to her was "Those breasts of yours, oh, those breasts of yours," but instead I said, "Could you tell her that I was here?"

"Fine," said the woman. "Fine, kid."

In the boat, in the middle of the river, I first heard the sound, and then I saw it. It came up like a steady, dense curtain, and the trees in the distance were white with it. When I lay on the boat bottom it coursed down my body, louder than before, raging, wet. Now it drummed on the retracted oars, the tin of the motor, it dripped in steady droplets from the nylon of the fishing line, and I was in the middle of it, stretched out on my back, in a T-shirt and pants, barefoot, hair long, eyes closed. When I opened them, it was still falling.

"Wisdom," announced my father, "is an important thing, but many are wise and few are smart."

"Probably," coughed Ruben Rubenović, the former textiles salesman, and touched his chin with trembling fingers.

"Rabbis," he added, "say that the heart is the best preacher, time the best teacher, the world the best book, and God your best friend."

My father, of course, begged to differ. "God?" he asked in an odd voice. "You can lose your faith in Him so quickly and get it back even quicker—is that a friend?" Uncle Ruben was quiet; mostly he kept quiet.

"Look, when a wise man sins," Father said with agitation and placed his hand on the table, "he figures he'll get away with it since he's wise, so he doesn't see he's been hoodwinked. Someone who's smart, of course, waits to see, and, most important, thinks."

"Chances are," coughed Uncle Ruben. "Rabbis say that yesterday is the past, today the future, and tomorrow is everybody's secret. Only God," he said in a soft voice, "knows secrets."

"And He never tells," agreed Father, caustically.

"He tells, my friend," countered Ruben Rubenović, "oh, He tells." And suddenly he'd laugh: "He tells them to the wise, and you are not wise—you're smart."

"Please," I said (I had gone to the door and come back to her bed), "are you sure you won't forget?" The woman lowered her arm, and her breast slid down like some selfish iceberg. "This really matters to me," I said, "so she'd know I was here."

"Kid," she said, "what's your name?"

Someone poked me gently when the teacher, a short, young woman with black hair, read my name out for the second time, and I found myself in front of a blackboard covered in tidy rows of numbers and symbols. They were chemical reactions; I recognized the reversible and irreversible processes though I was not looking at them. Standing there, I could see the roof of the neighboring army barracks and the Franciscan church belfry. The Tower, of course, was out of sight, but if I moved over some, for instance, if I were to take one step and get that eraser . . . Maybe.

"So," said the teacher, "do you know or not?"

I said nothing. I could feel two beads of sweat form on my forehead. Everyone could feel them. I'd heard others talk about how it was a treat to watch me when I had to answer in class. They spoke of some special sequence of perspiration zones on my face: first my forehead, then my upper lip, then droplets on my cheeks and clusters on my chin. I looked at the teacher; her eyes said exactly what I feared—and she knew it. She was staring straight at my upper lip and waiting for that colorless fluid, and once she'd spotted it she would glance over at my cheeks, wondering, perhaps, left or right? And she'd opt for gentle, almost imperceptible eye movements. Left, right. Left, right.

"I think you don't know," she said. "I think this time you really don't."

"I don't," I said.

"Good," she said, "fair enough."

I nodded.

"Go to your seat," she said, without looking at me. She entered the grade into the grade sheet. "Go to your seat," she said again, and I put the chalk back on the desk.

"It's methane," I said, nearly whispering. "Methane."

She started and looked over at me, astonished.

I was staring at the Tower.

"Is this age?" I wondered. Mother stubbornly refused our suggestion that she sleep later on Sundays, but she would linger in bed if my sister brought her coffee. Those first years, ones with short, mild winters, the river flowed right beyond the windowsill, and Mother justified her early rising by the murmuring sound that disturbed her sleep. Later, when the winters got longer and harsher, I began to get lonesome. The river was far off, it vanished into soft, funnel-shaped clouds of fog, and Mother had clearly begun to age.

"Is that age?" I'd wonder when I caught sight of her face in the morning. On it, with unconcealed horror, I'd see fresh, new wrinkles, broad and open, like cuts, or deft incisions of a surgical instrument. I was twenty-three years old at the time. I was lonely and dreamed about travel, about the people I'd meet. White expanses circled in my heart. The river that winter was covered with ice; it tumbled into hibernation like an old bear and vanished like the thin line of the horizon. The sparrows thinned out in January. It was a real challenge to lure two or three to the railing of the balcony with crumbs of fresh bread. I never saw my father in those days, or when I did these were short moments, moments of rest rather than readiness to talk.

"Is that age?" I wondered. He would come back exhausted from the hospital, his lips purple on a bloodless countenance. "It is a sin," I'd think, "not to retire such a man" (such a graying man—that was my idea), because my father was already sixty-seven. He had come dangerously close to death three or four times with his heart and gallbladder, and, regardless of my faith in the human race, I believed that people were trying to kill him. He slept every afternoon, on his hip, his hands raised above his head. Of course, my sister was here: she had wide hips and a blond fiancé, a Catholic. We hadn't insisted on a Jew—Mother and I hadn't; every now and then Father would mumble a few sentences about the beauties of the Jewish rites, the sanctity of the air through which the melodic voice of prayer meandered, and the indestructibility of the flame on the Sabbath candles. I think that we weren't really Jews then, those first years, when the winters were short and mild, when it seemed as if we were getting nearer to the river and not that it was fleeing from us. But later, when the winters got longer and harsher, we began to quibble.

"We are not indestructible," said Father, and he frowned at the mention of a storm.

"Is that age?" I wondered. Thick branches and birds'

nests floated along the river, and in April, when it rose after spring rains, I walked along it, deep in thought. My recent strolls with my father went on beyond autumn, the steps at Radecki had lost the firmness they'd had under people's feet, the fishermen came out late onto the water, and their wives stopped tying their hair in kerchiefs. I started noticing spring.

It was still raining when I stood up. It was moving toward Belgrade, and swimmers were scampering, frightened, around the island. The green foliage of the other shore glistened in the returning rays of sun. Rainbows dripped from leaves and church bells rang. "One morning," I mused, "I won't wake up." The city began, invisibly, to spread. It was a Sunday, a solemn, rainy, swollen day.

"Kid," she repeated, "what is your name? What do they call you?"

Now everything is fancy and shiny: a new floor in a new building. Nothing is left of the old hospital, though the guards are the same and greet me with a nod. But the odors! Have they changed? Earlier I used to walk through the gate into the yard—the guards did wave—inhaling deeply all the way to the broad white steps the unprotected fragrance of the park: I could hear birds and people's footsteps. Then twenty-odd steps in the corridor itself, a nurse in front of a temporary, patchily painted door, always the question "How is your mother?"—and the odors. I'd close the door behind me and find myself engulfed in their trusty strength. Whether I walked toward the freight elevator or took the stairs, they were undiminished: the same gaseous satiation, I thought. The walls were painted with shiny paint; it looked as though I'd get stuck to them if I brushed them. I walked along the middle of the worn staircase, and the nurses bumped into me without meaning to as they walked by. Father worked on the second floor, all the way to the left, and I'd find him in the high-ceilinged, white doctors' lounge. He was panting with exhaustion.

"Listen," I said (and I wondered: When did conjunctivitis encroach on my father's eyes? Which evening was it that Mother's veins began to swell? In which autumns did my sister's hips get bigger? When did I start noticing breasts?), "I only want you to tell her that I was here, that I came. She will be glad." Then I started for the door.

"Fine," she said. She followed me with her eyes, turning her head slowly, until I went out into the corridor. Then I heard her shouting: she was at the window when I passed through the yard. And further down, on Vuk Street and at the park gate, and later, by the high school and in front of the Air Force Hall; even the next day I could have sworn that I heard her, that I could divine her thoughts.

"Kid," she was calling, "kid, you didn't tell me your name!"

■ □ ■ □ ■

THE STORIES WE TELL

Me: On Mr. Frank the Watchmaker

ON TUESDAYS AND FRIDAYS, AFTER THEY'D SHOWN MOVIES ON television, Father would have nightmares, and I, barefoot, would bring him a glass of mineral water; he would thank me with empty eyes, chronically plagued by conjunctivitis, making no effort to grope for his glasses. The bedroom was the only fully furnished room then: a double bed, a larger and a smaller armoire, bedside tables, a mirror, a table and two chairs; everything of pale walnut, with an inlay of white ash and embellishments in rosewood in the shape of entwined Chinese dragons. There was a clock that went with the set, though it hadn't worked for years. "The gears wore down," said Mr. Frank, the watchmaker from Zmaj Jovanova Street. "No use repairing that." And we believed him. Watchmaker Frank had an assistant at the time, a skillful young man born in Srem, under whose fingertips layers of rust would fade. "It's not worth it," said the assistant, "though you could replace the whole works inside, but then," he shook his head, "then it would be an altogether different clock." Father had demanded, you see, that the clock keep its ancient chime, of which we were especially fond. "It wouldn't have its old ticktock?" asked Father. "No," answered Mr. Frank, "it would not." So the clock just stood there, like a worn-out veteran, on a shelf in the larger armoire, and always, almost unnoticeably, showed that the time was four in the afternoon.

Father: On Milosavljević the Dentist

With us in Ć., while we were living there, one of our most regular acquaintances was a dentist, Milosavljević, a Seventh-Day Adventist. When we moved there from Peć, he believed (since he was familiar with the history of religion) that there were certain things he shared with us. He soon noticed, however, that I did not observe the Sabbath, that I would accept shifts at the hospital even on that holy day. So when, after a few weeks, he bumped into me at the Mikić Bridge, he kept me there in a lengthy conversation about faith and how to respect it. I told him that I am not religious, but that I used to believe. "Believe? In what?" asked Milosavljević. "In people," I said, which did not satisfy him. I mentioned as I was leaving that these last few nights I'd been praying, to myself of course, without following any particular rules. "Like an ordinary Happy Birthday," he said, and I had to agree.

Me: On a Synagogue in Ć.

In 1950 we were the only Jewish family in Ć., and it was perfectly natural, Father said, that no one was about to build us a synagogue. So Mother dared to go to church whenever she felt like it, and we celebrated St. Simeon's saint's day, and we prepared wheat in the Serbian Orthodox way and had cake for the feast. Father got infectious jaundice on top of everything, and he was taken to a clinic in Belgrade in an ambulance. "One disaster follows another," Mother said, and my sister—just as we'd expected—came down with a mild case of pneumonia. I wandered away from home twice that summer. The police patrols found me when I was visiting Mr.

Drago, head of the freight office at the train station, where I had been inquiring in a solemn voice: "Why don't trains have feet?" Later, in the winter of 1954, we moved to Zemun, where there were a few more Jews, but most of them old and feeble. Half-dead, you might say.

Father: On Mr. Demayo's Widow

When your mother and I, after the war, as soon as we'd married, went to pick up our bedroom furniture at Gospodar-Jevremova Street, the door was opened for us by Mr. Demayo's widow. Those years, when statistics had just appeared as a significant science, one never knew who should be conveying condolences to whom. So we were led in silence into a small, dark room where, neatly piled, stood the entire set of furnishings: a complete bedroom made of walnut. This was Mother's furniture, and I was amazed. I touched the wood and talked about matching colors on the walls. At that time it was rather bold to speak of wallpaper, but I did speak of it, wallpaper the color of a calm sky, I said, and Demayo's widow remembered that a cousin of hers had had that kind. I had met her in Zagreb, and I said that everything there was different, that I knew that because I had studied there and lived there a while, on Nad Lipom Street, at number 3. "Yes," said Mrs. Demayo, "that is how it was here, too, but the damp got to it, and the bombs fell." "I remember Dorćol," I said, "but by then I was knee-deep in the Timok River." "Ah, yes," said the widow, though I doubt she believed me. She had earrings with diamonds and long, slender fingers. There wasn't a piano there, in the house. "Yes," she repeated, and consented to take food coupons and three packages of scented soap instead of cash. The bottle of cologne your mother offered at the end she flatly refused to accept. Though she did so, I am certain, with trembling nostrils, plunging her long, slender fingers into her hair.

Me: On the Chorus from the Zagreb Home for the Elderly

At the Belgrade Jewish Center we used to get packages of candy and American chocolate for celebrations of Hanukkah and Rosh Hashanah, and sometimes the chorus from the Zagreb Home for the Elderly would perform. That must be how we decided we'd spend our summer at the Jewish summer camp in Rovinj, where I learned to swim, even in water over my head. Of the ten of us who were staying in bunk beds, I was the only one who was circumcised. The others—Darko Vajs, David Levi, Mladen Štrumberger, Aca Kabiljo, Stevan Novković, Josip Perera, Damir Štajn, Igor Mišić, Miša Biro—clustered together and stared at my wrinkled, bare, little penis. Frightened, I thought it was visibly different than the others, even in the dark. The actual rite of circumcision, *brit milah,* took place in Priština, before a bevy of guests. That day, the eighth day after I was born, while staring at the pink place upon which the *mohel* was making his final incisions, Aunt Mucika and Aunt Elza resolved to leave Yugoslavia, and Uncle Jakov and Uncle Gideon obeyed. Two years after my summer in Rovinj, when the camp moved down to Split, we began getting packages of coffee and clothing from Brazil, with dried oranges and succulent dates from Israel. We sent them packages, too. We stuffed these with useless odds and ends from crafts stores, things that were not utilitarian but only for decoration. And for remembering.

Me: On Life in Zemun

That is how it always was in our apartment. In the beginning, when we first moved to Zemun, we didn't know a soul. We were used to the friends who had crowded into our apartment in Ć.; we paced around our single room, aimlessly, until twilight. In the dark—Mother hadn't stopped smoking then, and the tip of her cigarette would move, as if enchanted, of its own volition—we'd try to recognize one another by the creaking parquet floor, and we'd bump into each other and apologize in artificial tones, as if we were strangers. That is what people are like, after all, when they are lonely. There were people like that in Ć. But in a small town people all live the same life. Father, you mustn't forget, was a prominent figure, the first gynecologist in the entire Morava River Valley, and from the carriages, driven by horses and oxen, bells jingled in friendly greetings as we walked along the streets of Ć. On the days when new movies came to the movie theater, we'd go and sit in the reserved seats. Sometimes the darkness would be interrupted, the lights would go up, and a voice could be heard: Doctor, they need you at the hospital! Doctor! And off Father would go. That is how we lived in Ć. Who could have imagined that life in Zemun would be different? Father was still a gynecologist, we still went to the movies, people would say hello on the streets, but there were people there I didn't know, and not everyone gave up their seat to Mother. What could we possibly have been expecting?

Father: On My Birth in Peć

"I'd rather," I told your mother, "that his name doesn't remind me of this whole war." You were there, whimpering in her arms. We got by during those years as best we knew how, and if we hadn't done so well at communicating with the Albanians in whose house we lived, who knows where you would have been born. We were genuinely poor. I bought *The Collected Works of Dostoevsky* and had to do without meat for several days. "I really don't want," I repeated to your mother, "his name to remind me of anything." "Fine," said Mother. When she started to breast-feed you, your sister, though she was plenty old enough to prefer solid food, grabbed the other breast and wouldn't let go. She'd trot around lugging this little footstool, and shouting: "The other's for me! The other's for me!" We gave her my mother's name, and that settled things with my ancestors. "Fine," agreed your mother, and in the evening, by the light of the kerosene lamp, I took up the Bible and let it fall open by itself. David was the first name on the left-hand side. By that time we were running late, so we entered you under the wrong day at the registrar's to avoid paying the fine. That's why you're thirteen days younger; you'll live thirteen days longer than everyone else. For you, I stole from death. Only later did I find out about Absalom.

Me: On the Death of Father's Sister

Though we thought it might be, the last letter from Brazil was not edged in black, but still it brought sad news. Father changed and, all of a sudden, discovered religion. He'd light candles at dusk and sing sad prayers with an atonal voice; his eyes were red, swollen under his glasses. For forty days you weren't supposed to cook anything, but he'd grown accustomed to Christianity; he'd tried Mother's flavorful cooking, and he shortchanged his religion. He gave up cholent eggs, banicika cheese rolls, and "pastel" meat pies for a good dish of sauerkraut and thick, homemade soups. Poor Mucika, he'd mutter with a sigh, and he'd cry, his nose running as if he were a kid. My sister Berta hung her gift, a slender Moses made of gold, on a chain. After forty days, Father was calmer, though silence was the only thing he'd speak, and brood, about.

Me: On My Schoolteacher Violeta

On Sundays, my mother would put a flower in her hair and light the candles on the table in the dining room. When I'd surprise her in front of the mirror, deep lakes of fragrance came from behind her ears. Under her lipstick, I knew her lips were even redder than they looked. In the evening, the guests would begin to arrive. The director of the hospital would sweep his hat off with a gallant gesture and kiss my mother's hand. "He is such a dear man," Mother would say, and she'd hurry to greet the new guest, Mr. Filipović, who'd come from neighboring S. in a cab pulled by two white horses. He tweaked off his clean white gloves, and, with his face ruddy from the wind, he bowed deeply to Mother and my sister. Then the director of the local forestry office stepped in front of me and held my hand for a long while, inquiring in a soft voice about school, my grades, the little girls. Childhood is like a doe, he said, so fragile, they're murdering it every day. Lieutenant Janovski whispered to Mother in confidence that his wife would be arriving shortly with their daughter, that they were late in getting dressed though they lived right next door. Mrs. Pavić, wife of the late bank owner, patted my head: Good evening, young man, she'd say, and she would move away with a merciless rustle of her ball gown. There were others, always one or two new faces, while some of the older, familiar ones disappeared. Then they embarked on the first course in silence, strictly measured by the ticking of the wall clock. Last of all, out of breath, constantly apologizing, my teacher arrived, all in blue. Miss Violeta, my mother would say, you are late again, and she would smile and accept the proffered hand of the director of the hospital. Really, she'd say, I'm so terribly sorry, and Milka, wearing a white apron, would put a bowl of soup on the table. Could Miss Violeta hear how my heart was pounding? You say nothing and you don't know.

Me: On My First Conversation with Father

The first serious conversation we had was when I was fourteen. When you saw me stark naked, still damp from my bath, you and Mother quibbled about whether I had a hernia or not. When she left, while I was putting on my clean underwear, you started talking in a weary voice about women. I looked into your eyes and realized that you were old. The next day you tested me on everything, as if I were a restless student: I didn't know the role of progesterone, and you waved me away in dismissal, disgruntled. You learn about women while you're young, you said, and we never uttered a word about this again.

Father: On the True Order of Things

What is going on with you? I asked myself around that time, and you were reading Heraclitus. During dinner, you championed his thought that war is the father of all things, but we were not prepared to embark on a conversation. Your sister was tired, your mother—when the seamstress is in the house—refuses to think; between you and me, ever since the June war, there had been a wall of indifferent silence. Adroitly, darting glances at me, you claimed that Jews had been saved by wars and genocide, and that after these exterminations—since they were forced to mingle with the goyim—they managed to rejuvenate their genes, to get stronger. You provoked a rage in me such as I'd never known before. I was ready to order you in a sharp voice to stop bringing such stories to the table, to shut up; I wanted to teach you a lesson. Calmly, in a softer voice, you went on: Are people still believers if they betray their faith in order to save their lives? Does a clandestine return to their own faith purify them? I know what you were talking about—the age of the Inquisition and the Marranos; you were secretly accusing me of being a Christian. Then I understood that you'd been reading books I had never even heard of and a sense of serenity spread through me: I acknowledged you. In the evening, in bed, words of forgotten prayers were clear in my memory. When we talk about the true order of things, I will tell you my sincere opinion of the position of the living and the nonliving in the universe. Meanwhile, I fell asleep.

Me: On the First Star

My love, Marina, took me by the hand and led me to the rose garden. Outside the tall gate, the street was quiet and full of darkness. We sat on the marble steps and intently watched the sky. The small and larger roses wafted fragrance, and the night descended upon us. When we caught sight of the first star, we'd kiss each other on the cheek in delight. I was five, she was four.

Me: On the Night

Sometimes my father would watch me while I studied by the hearth. He'd offer to help. Suddenly we'd be talking about completely insignificant things. We'd mention the spring winds in the branches and forgotten wars. Father would fall silent, amazed. He said that I was like him, that I enjoyed studying. Mostly, I was listening closely. I was getting used to the new city. Ć., with its bridges, had sunk into the river. I'd discovered the Kalemegdan fortress in Belgrade, but didn't dare explore it. I felt like a wary seafarer, and would urge Father to talk about Columbus. He would bring home almanacs and children's magazines from time to time. It looked as if my future was already told, that everyone but me knew what I'd do and where I'd live. To my disappointment, those born under the sign of Pisces are supposed to have brilliant careers in a law office. I so wanted to be an admiral. Even when I'm not studying, I think about the river. "What is it?" asked Father. I start talking about the Danube, but he looks down, goes back to reading his paper. I don't think he's listening to me. I stop talking. Deep in the night, when I think, I am truly happy.

Me: On Quarrels

Mother is holding her tongue while she is bent over the washtub. One could say she's listening. When Father stops shouting, she wipes her hands for a while on her apron, and turns so we don't see her tears. The next morning she makes terrible coffee, and Father accepts her revenge as inevitable punishment—he sips the hot liquid with a bowed head and keeps a gentle expression on his face. In front of the temple, leaning on me, he is incomparably older: he says nothing, he's silent and ponders. That is how they endure: they punish one another, first with a human hand, then with the Lord's hand.

Father: On Hypnosis of the Buttocks

It isn't all about how you hold the hypodermic or how precisely you open the ampules. The skill is in the shot. I tap the patient's buttock first, I slap it a few times, quickly, with my hand, and then immediately, while the person still hasn't started feeling, I plunge in the needle. It is a strong thrust that breaks the skin. Without waiting, without thinking, I press my thumb and the fluid spreads through the body. I pull out the needle. The patient only reacts, believe it or not, when I swab her with a cotton ball moistened with iodine or alcohol. Meanwhile, you can be sure, she has no idea what has happened to her. She'll know later.

Me: On My First Demons

"Will you look at that?" Father would exclaim whenever he didn't find a book in its place. "Do you still believe that there are no demons or evil spirits?" he'd ask me. It made no difference that he found the book right nearby, behind a pillow or under the newspaper. He kept at it obstinately, his hair grew gray, especially in the evenings, when we lit the lamps.

Me: On Sexual Maturity

Mother bathed us one by one: first me, then my sister, then Father at the end. I used to get undressed in front of her without the slightest twinge of shame. She'd kneel, add wood to the water heater. "Get in," she'd say, and she'd rub me all over my body. But one day, while I was sitting in the bathtub, she dropped the sponge down between my legs and said: "From now on you'll wash down there by yourself."

Father: On Frugality

There are some things you've never mastered: you can't ride a bicycle, you don't know how to ice skate, you can't stand roller skates, you get sick in buses. Back when you wanted a tricycle, I couldn't afford to buy you one. Later, you got too big for it. Now I'd get it for you, just so you'd have it. But, alas, it seems you've learned to be frugal; you'd be furious at me for wasting the money. I know that you'll refuse my offer to get you a new coat or shoes. I set aside the money just in case you say yes, but I no longer expect you will. When you say, No thank you, I don't need anything, I know that you are my son. Frugality may not be a virtue, but, when it gets passed down from one generation to the next, it isn't a fault either. Not a day goes by, you know, that I don't wonder: Will you, too, have a son?

Me: On the First Days of Winter

On the first days of winter we would cheerfully keep the doors closed. Father would cram his pockets with handkerchiefs, Mother would avoid colds and pneumonia in magnificent style. When the alarm clock rang in the morning, we would hesitate. Much later, when we got up, my sister would talk quite seriously at breakfast about getting engaged. We drank Russian tea.

Me: On the First Dog

When I am my most determined, my memories go back only to the dead end in Ć. and never any further. Then I was three or four years old. They took me for walks across the Mikić Bridge and let me play in the front yard. In the garden I'd always snap the flowers, especially the tulips. One dog, now very indistinctly remembered, had white fur and an ornate tail. But I can't for the life of me remember its name! If I say Jackie, what I see is an all-black snout, black eyes, and a shamelessly naked rear end—and that's not him. That must mean that we'd gotten a second dog.

Me: On the Necessity of Sleep

Mother got up from time to time and painfully rubbed her shoulders. Though she got shots and took vitamins, immobility was gradually taking over. There were days when she longed endlessly for sleep, and Father, reclining in the chair, under the luxury of the old-fashioned chandelier, was watching television series late into the night. Mother would bury her face in her pillow, wrap herself up in her quilt, sleep right against the wall, but the light would find her eyelids by some hidden path. Like the heroes of the great tragedies, Mother would sit up in bed and shout: "Turn out that light, God help you!" and then in a softer voice she'd add: "I need my sleep."

Father: On Mother's Lips

This is the way I was thinking: If it turns out to be a girl, Lord, let me give her, without a trace of anger, the name Louisa. But you were born instead. Your mother's water broke in the cab on the way to the hospital. I told the cabby: "Flog the ass!" "Can't do that, doctor," he replied. "That's a sin." The next day the rumor spread through Peć that my wife had had a son. You will never make me—so don't even try—tell you how I felt and whom all I thanked. I spent one entire afternoon in the shade of a spreading pear tree that used to bear big, juicy fruit. It would make you think about lips, and I did.

Me: On Moments of Loneliness

In moments of pure loneliness I would press my face to the windowpane and watch the arrival of the bus. Nothing could stop me from believing: the next arrival is the real one, the master of your destiny will be coming. No one ever did. Heavy droplets formed from my breath, then slid down, leaving behind them a slender, silvery trace much like the track left by a snail's foot. When I'd turn around, without looking I knew: Father would be reading the paper, Mother would be knitting, my sister would be standing in front of the mirror. Everything smelled of uniformity: the afternoon coffee, the evening news on television at 6:30, the walk out to the quay an hour later. I would come back tired from the walk, thinking of the moon and its reflection in the river. In the rooms you could smell the fresh bedclothes and the intoxication of sleep. Father dozed in his chair, so he could not hear the door creak. Mother started, frightened: "Good Lord," she'd say, "I've told him a thousand times to go to bed. Why is he torturing himself?" "And not only himself," I'd answer. But Father would wake up suddenly, he'd look at the screen. "Oh," he'd say, "they've killed someone again! Those poor people."

Me: On the Need for Escape

Sometimes I go to the hotel lawn, I throw back my head and stand there: I can feel the stars right down to my bones. In a flash, without looking, I see myself: a minuscule dot on the slightly larger speck of Earth that is hurtling pointlessly through the universe, running a race with no goal. I catch myself, like a drowning man, at that word "pointless." I tell myself, while pain wracks my flung-back head, how pointless it is to feel "pointlessness," how I have already done so much, how I am still young. That is my last resort: my youth. But the bags under my eyes, the rheumatic pains before the rainy season begins, stab me in the region of my heart. You have to escape. Yet when I open my eyes, I see that even the stars have tricked me. There is only one here or there, gleaming through rushing clouds, dangling carelessly beneath the blackened sky, then vanishing. But somehow I believe in stars, in polestars. How could I do without them? Where would I go? I walk, slowly, home.

Me: On the Homeland

One morning I sent him a dream about Jerusalem, and I could hear how he was softly, secretly, crying. We still didn't know then that the war would break out soon and that the city would be united, just as we didn't know that we'd visit it, first him in a few years, and later me. When I came back, we held each other for a long time, as if desperate, not even closing the front door. And while the neighbors caroused, we confessed to each other our failure, our longing, and our passion to return. "You have watered Zion with your tears," Mother used to say. Because we knew that we'd stay here, for good. In our homeland.

■ □ ■ □ ■

THE GOSPEL ACCORDING TO MY FATHER

AFTER INTERMINABLE AUTUMN FLOODING, THE RIVER RECEDED overnight, leaving behind it a bare, gaping space of muddy shores, and when we—Father, Ruben Rubenović, and I—taking advantage of the first sunny day, went out onto the quay, suddenly Father nearly sobbed, shut his eyes painfully, and leaned with his full weight on my arm. "What have they done," he gasped, "what have they done with the river?" And I could see his knees shaking.

"Let's sit down," said Ruben Rubenović, former textiles salesman, but Father refused to turn. He took off his glasses and stood there: his feet askew, his head drooping, his shoulders rounded. He rubbed his eyes with his thumb and middle finger, then his forehead, cheeks, lips. "I don't understand," he said, "I really can't understand. Why anyone would want . . . "

"Let's sit down," repeated Ruben Rubenović and took Father under the arm.

"I don't understand," said Father, turning to me. "You are always down here, you're always coming. What have they done with all that water?"

"I don't know," I said.

"Come on," said Ruben Rubenović and touched Father's shoulder, "sit down."

Father relaxed, went limp, his eyes filled with tears, his eyeglasses slid between his fingers. "Who did this," he glared nearsightedly into Ruben Rubenović's face, "who did this?"

"What's with you?" asked the former textiles salesman.

"What's with nature?" replied Father.

"Yes," said Ruben Rubenović, "what's with nature?"

Behind us, in the immediate vicinity, workers had descended on a half-demolished factory hall. You could hear the blows of mallets and the crash of falling girders.

"What is that?" Father spun around. "Who's making that racket?"

"They are demolishing the chocolate factory," I said.

"Maybe it was them," Father clutched my knee, "maybe it was them who did this to the river . . . Why don't you go? Ask them! Maybe they've diverted the flow . . . "

Ruben Rubenović picked up Father's glasses: "What's with you?" he asked. "What are you talking about?"

"About the river," Father shouted. "What have they done to the river?"

"With the river?" said Ruben Rubenović and looked around. The river had withdrawn, hidden in itself, suddenly laying bare the silty expanses of both shores. Forgotten boats wallowed on their sides, and poking out from among the larger and smaller rocks were branches, broken bottles, faded newspapers, cans. In the afternoon haze across the quay was the figure of a lone man out walking, a man with a hat and a small dog. Clouds were piling up over Belgrade, but above us shone the miserly winter sun. "The river is fine," Ruben Rubenović answered Father's question. "But you tell me what's with you."

Father wiped away the tears, took his glasses from the former textiles salesman, and peered through them around him: a man who has unexpectedly found himself in a strange place. "I don't know," he said. "Sometimes I sit like that with the little woman. I say nothing and I think about how everything is changing. I listen to the harsh blows of diggers, carpenters," he pointed behind his back, "and I think: don't worry, it's good, progress is happening, man is trying to get somewhere . . . But in the morning, when I leave for work, I stand still for a long time outside our front door, I don't know where I am, where I'm headed . . . I'd just as soon go back in . . . "

"That will pass," said Ruben Rubenović.

"My life will pass," said Father.

"What did you expect?"

Father said nothing.

On the other shore, among the underbrush, a car appeared. There was shouting and a dog barking, then the chuckle of a woman. Next to us, a little short-haired dog stopped and pricked up its ears.

"Come, Arnold," said the man with the hat, and we turned. "Lovely day," he smiled at us.

"It is nice," said Ruben Rubenović.

"The sun," said the man, "eh?" The dog sniffed our feet; he growled at my father. "Come, Arnold!" shouted the man with the hat and whistled. Father shooed the dog away; it backed up a few steps and barked loudly. Barking resounded from the other shore.

"Nothing can help with that," said the former textiles salesman and gently smoothed my father's hand. "You're hoping in vain."

"I am not hoping," said Father. "What is there to place my hopes in?"

"I was wondering that myself," said Ruben Rubenović.

"In him?" said Father and glances at me.

"For one."

"And what else?"

"Your wife. Your daughter."

"And you?" said Father. "You have no one. What do you place your hopes in?"

Ruben Rubenović gestures unspecifically, but in the general direction of the skies. "In nothing." And then he added, at once: "In everything."

"In God?" I asked.

Ruben Rubenović studied the skies, the river; he pondered: "Maybe."

"Huh," said Father.

We sat there, quiet. Behind the island appeared a barge moving lugubriously, then tugboats lined up. People bustled around on deck, bells rang, whistles and sharp curses were heard.

"Isn't the water level a little low?" asked Father.

"They know," I said. "They have markers, lines, lanterns, everything they need."

"At night they navigate, too?"

"Yes," I confirmed.

"Courage," said my father.

"Yes."

"I hear," coughed Ruben Rubenović, "that you have been inquiring, of late, about Jesus. Is that correct?"

"Who told you that?"

"So it is correct."

"Who told you that?" I repeated.

"I heard," said the former textiles merchant. "It doesn't matter where."

"Do they take their wives with them?" asked my father.

"Who? Where?"

"The bargemen," said Father. "On their trips, when they navigate."

"It's time you started doubting," said Ruben Rubenović without looking at me, "but watch that your conscience doesn't get to you. Doubting won't hurt."

"Why would my conscience get to me?" I said. "History has proven . . . "

"If I hate something," said my father, "it's history."

"You are right," said Ruben Rubenović. "Until the time when it will be up to historians to establish some truth."

"Artificial," said Father.

"Precisely," agreed the former textiles salesman, "artificial, yes. Until such a time history means nothing. In the best case, it becomes a weapon, but a weapon . . . "

"History speaks for itself alone," I said.

"Like time," said my father.

"History *is* time."

"But time cannot be recorded."

"Why do you believe in it then?" Ruben Rubenović asked me.

I said nothing.

"Do your doubting without textbooks, follow the spirit."

"It seems to me that's the way he is doubting," Father said.

"How would you know?"

"I read what he writes. He gives it to me sometimes."

"Then don't talk about it," frowned Ruben Rubenović. "Doubt! How do you doubt!"

I shrugged.

"Would you rather become a Christian?"

Father looked at me.

"Well," I said.

"Yes or no?"

"Depends," I said, "on the situation."

"You're on the fence," said Father.

"You used to criticize the Spanish Marranos," Ruben Rubenović reminded me, "and now you are suggesting that, depending on the situation, you might change your faith? How come?"

"I am not much of a believer," I said.

"The soul, my son, the soul."

The man with the hat and the little dog walked back by us, and we stopped talking. The dog sniffed our feet again, and again, disgruntled by something, it barked at Father. "Arnold, come," called the man.

"Going home so soon?" asked Ruben Rubenović.

"Well," said the man, "plenty for now. A little stroll before dinner."

"Yes, indeed."

"Good-bye," said my father.

We stopped talking again, faced with the river. We didn't turn, but it seemed as if the clouds had caught up with the sun: it was getting gloomier and cooler, a chilly breeze began blowing. Behind us, the racket continued with unabated ferocity: the echoes of blows alternated with the dull thud of falling debris. The air smelled like dust.

"Those are hellish jobs," said Father. "Barges, explosives, forests, no family, forever on the move—I cannot imagine how those people survive!"

"Eh," said Ruben Rubenović and turned around. "Should we be getting back?"

"I'd rather not," I said.

"We'll stay," said Father. "After all, we don't even take the same ways back."

Ruben Rubenović got up; he started buttoning up his old winter coat. "By the waters of the Danube," he said, "we sat and we wept, but what was it we remembered?" And then he left, without a word in parting, thumping his cane dully around him.

"Will you be stopping by this afternoon?" Father called after him, but he didn't answer. "What's wrong with him?"

"Most likely he longs," I said, "to hear the harps."

"Is that from some psalm?"

"Yes."

"Are you being nasty?"

We exchanged glances.

"He threw you with that question about the Marranos," said Father. "Admit it."

"What can I say?"

Father sighed, stood up, pushed his hands into the pockets of his coat.

"You've been different recently," he said. He didn't look at me.

"I don't know," I said, "I really don't know."

"What do you think about when Mother lights the candles on the Sabbath?"

"What about you?"

"I pray."

"Me, too," I said.

Father took several steps, strode down the concrete stairs. "Someone has ruined this river," he said, "but I just don't know who." He kept going down, without turning, and rapidly disappeared below the edge of the sidewalk. A little later I caught sight of him as he was gingerly skirting the shallow puddles and slimy mud, approaching the water's edge. It occurred to me that I should warn him: after all, his age, his obvious clumsiness, and the riverbed so slippery! But he kept moving along, persistently, avoiding obstacles, and when I thought he'd already gotten his shoes, feet, and pants soaked, he began to walk upon the water. The river shivered under the weight, waves rippled the surface; Father spread out his hands like a tightrope walker and then proceeded more surely, more and more confident in his own sense of balance. In vain, horrified, I closed my eyes. He advanced over the agitated surface, serene, firm, going further and further, his face to the wind, through the storm, the sleet, until he got across to the other shore and collapsed, utterly exhausted, on the dirty surface of sand. And there he sat, leaning on his elbows, panting, but still, from time to time, he found the strength to wave to me and call in an unexpectedly clear voice.

"Cross over," he called. "Cross over already! Come on, cross the river!"

■ □ ■ □ ■

MAMA

Introduction.

A FEW DAYS AFTER MY SISTER'S WEDDING MOTHER BEGAN talking to things. At first she only addressed the carnations or the yellow roses while she changed the water. Later, when spring had begun, the yard was turning green, and the plum tree was all in flowers, she'd embark on long, monotonous debates with the cutlery. She talked (you could hear her from behind the kitchen door) about her rough life, but she wasn't complaining, she didn't mind. She brought forth, calmly, in a half-whisper, facts, information. Sometimes she would halt to remember, and then she spoke softly, with pauses, probably frowning with the effort—because memory had already begun to elude her; memories melted and escaped into dreams. At that time, after my sister's wedding, she was a full sixty years old, her varicose veins bothered her, her joints, too; it looked like she would never recover. At the end of the summer she went to a health spa, despite this. She wrote us two or three times. She sent a postcard on which you could clearly see the warm-water baths, a neat lawn, convalescents out for a stroll. She came back visibly improved, her cheeks fuller, her hair lighter in color. She stopped in the doorway and kissed my father on the cheek. Then she touched the kitchen table, the stove. "How are you?" she asked. "What have you been up to?" And we knew she was not addressing us.

The First Conversation with Things. Father.

As far as I know, if my memory does not fail me, it happened the next Monday, eight days after the wedding. The last guests had left the house by then, and the little woman, chances are, must have felt a sudden loneliness. She was our daughter, after all, not someone else's. She spent twenty-six years with us, a third of a lifetime, her whole childhood. Sooner or later, one of us would surely have started talking to things. Maybe we do—it wouldn't surprise me. We just happened to notice how the little woman was doing that, so we diverted attention from ourselves. Otherwise, from the medical standpoint, what we have here is exhaustion, loneliness, overtaxed nerves. This is not my specialty, I am a gynecologist, but I'd recommend rest, relaxation, long walks. A health spa? Yes, a health spa, too.

Faded Carnations. Description.

In a small vase, cut crystal, half-transparent, with long handles, there are three of them. The largest blossom is still open, the petals only slightly wrinkled, darker. The middle one looks sooty, scorched. The smallest is devastated, muted red. Time had, therefore, done its job. They are twisted, turned in the same direction. No one looks after them anymore. The water (though we cannot see the water!) is stagnant, spread with a thin layer of scum, surprising the nostrils with its musty stench. In front of the vase is a three-pronged candleholder and several family photographs in the same (cheap, plastic, commercial: LEK, Ljubljana) frame. The magnified expanse includes the desk with a series of details; and then: the corner of the room, the room itself; and in the background: the two-bedroom apartment, the five-story postwar building, the awkward square, the entrance into town, the town itself; and so on: the suburbs, a nearby hill, the wooded plains and sandy stretches, both shores of the river, glades and scrub brush, the autonomous province; and faster and faster: the republic, the whole country, now it's already the continent, oceans, unexplored realms of South America, new expeditions to the poles; and in the end: the whole earth, the bluish ball, which lazily, with a certain indecisiveness, is spinning through the cosmos.

Yellow Roses.

This is a separate story. Is there anyone who still brings yellow roses on the day of a wedding? You only see something like that in the movies and popular songs, never in real life. Imagine bringing yellow roses when you know that every one of the rest of the hundred or more invited guests will be bringing carnations or red roses or expensive baskets of flowers. But Evangelina arrives, nonetheless, with a bouquet of yellow roses, with an enormous bouquet, without the white wrapping paper, filling her arms. She comes into the reception hall at the Yugoslav Air Force Hall precisely when the party is at its liveliest, when the bride and groom, awkwardly clutching the wide handle of a knife, are trying to slice the wedding cake. And now, of course, all eyes turn to her, talk dies, the music dies, until she steps, quite lightly, one foot in front of the other, the full length of the room to the head of the table where the bride and groom, still bent over, are hovering unconvincingly over the fancy cake with the knife. Then Evangelina spreads her arms, raises them high as if she is giving a sign to the musicians, and the yellow roses scatter all around the hall. In the burst of dizzying hubbub, the groom tries in vain to say something; the orchestra, however, repeats a long, vigorous flourish. Then the young married couple, pink dolls in a tuxedo and a lacy dress, begin to wobble almost unnoticeably. They topple flat on their faces into the rich sweet-shop frosting: snow-white and (you sense) overly sweetened whipped cream.

Spring in the Yard, through the Kitchen Window. Mother.

The blossoming plum tree in the yard, suddenly green. In the yard that the tenant council has been trying for years, in vain, to turn into a flowering garden, with titmice and a summer pavilion, I assume, and goldfinches in the shrubbery. Like the neighboring building's garden, where the former mayor is now learning how to walk again. I know that it is cruel to think of someone only when misfortune strikes, but when are you otherwise likely to remember them? The boys always trample everything: they pull up saplings, break off newly sprouted branches, play soccer, gallivant. And the sparrows? The sparrows probably peck at the seeds. After all, what would boys want with seeds? The mayor has had a stroke, a traffic accident or some such thing. I see him as he walks, now, in the spring: back and forth, back and forth, from wall to wall. All day long his lips are moving. He's probably speaking, testing himself. I heard that he even forgot words, all the letters, the entire alphabet. And how old could he be, anyway? Fifty? Maybe he's fifty, with a wife and a child.

Vanity and Bureau.

She hid, my sister, in the bedroom. She sat there, perfectly pale, in front of the old vanity and silently studied herself in the mirror. We thought she'd cry, but only her lips quivered now and then, and two lines creased her cheeks. She was ready to go at eight o'clock, though the wedding procession wasn't coming for her until ten, maybe a little earlier, it is hard to say. Father crossed his arms in the dining room, leaning over, listening for any footsteps in the stairwell. He tiptoed, from time to time, over to the bedroom, and from the doorway offered words and smiles to soothe. Then my sister lowered her veil, as if she wanted to hide her face, and stood up. From somewhere came the sound of a bell ringing, and absolutely unknown people jostled into the front hall. My sister started, turned, raised her hand, and gently, without moving at all, touched the smooth surface of the bureau, stealthily, but with love. And then they took her, in classic silence, which was broken not by the noise of a cannon or any firearm (if that is what you were expecting), but by the sound, just as trusty, of smashed crystal and a merciless stain of red wine spreading with unreachable speed across the polished parquet floor. Except for my mother and, in part, for me, however, no one paid it the slightest mind. Those nearest tried to touch my sister's white wedding dress, and the furthest, with effort, stood on their tiptoes. Presently, the day was done.

Behind the Kitchen Door. Father.

I know that it wasn't fair, don't hold it against me, but sometimes, if you want to help people, you need to rely on things that, in ordinary life, disgust us. As long as life is ordinary, of course, but that is another subject; I won't digress. I can only explain. I went out of the kitchen one day, after lunch, tired, probably sleepy, and she began to talk before I'd closed the door behind me. First I thought that I should stoop because of the murky glass at the top of the door, which I did. Reconciled, I heard her voice, a half-whisper so to speak, though at first I couldn't make out the words. It all seemed like distant murmurs, humming, and reminded me of ancient rituals, even—if I may say so—of magic. Yes. However, as soon as I heard her steps, and when I could no longer determine with certainty where they were headed, I withdrew, not having figured anything out. I had to, because if she had opened the door by chance, she would have come upon me all bent over like that. I nearly had my ear to the keyhole—you can imagine! After all, this gray hair on my head . . . The next time, naturally, the words became clearer, the sentences acquired meaning: she was addressing the cutlery she had just washed, the knives, forks, spoons. Calmly, softly, simply she was retelling—*re*telling!—her life, without images, without sounds, only the facts, only the truth . . . And now, one cannot say much about that, for what is there to say? About life, I mean. About life that has come, whether we like it or not (I won't say), to its end (I'll say: as far as it could come).

Nothing? I agree. You have no idea how much I agree. Though, truth be told, sometimes, without shame, even when my son was with me, there, behind the kitchen door, I burst into tears, perhaps precisely because there was nothing to be said, that I could be only one thing: a mute witness, nothing more. But, you see, then we sent her off to the spa—we somehow managed to convince her at the end of the summer—and when she came back, the talking had stopped, at least the murmuring, but not that odd affection for things. When, for instance, she'd lower her chapped hand on the old kitchen cupboard—if you could have seen her eyes! . . . Though perhaps there may exist a reason, a genuine solution, cruel in its inevitability—so much so that I am almost afraid to ask you, but what do you think, anyway, regardless of everything: hasn't she, maybe, now, in her sixty-first year of age, lost her hope in people? Pardon?

Photographs Framed in an Advertisement. Description.

A total of four, the smallest of which was probably taken even before the war: such a young woman, with a nice smile, in a chintz dress. The largest photograph: the same woman again (we recognize her by her smile), though older, her hair swept back from her forehead, in (as far as we can tell) an embroidered blouse or light sweater with a broad collar draped carelessly over her twisted shoulders. Twisted, because in front of her stand (or sit) two children, a boy and a girl, hugging each other, staring: a. (the little girl) at the distance, the irretrievable distance above the photograph frame, serious, almost wise; and b. (the boy) straight into the camera lens, his head lowered, his eyebrows raised, with uncertainty and a completely certain mistrust. All three figures, regardless of their smiles, wisdom, and mistrust, have sad eyes—eyes which, if we turn our gaze to the picture in the left corner, we recognize again, this time those of a grown (in the picture) girl, with a long neck and hair up in a powerful bun, such as you surely recall from the first years of the sixties. The last photograph (if you're expecting the boy grown, you are wrong) is obviously not so old, taken using the classic method of the "express snapshot for passports and other documents"—in other words: the upper half of the photograph is the head, the lower half is the chest; smiling, though the smile is not genuine; a man about sixty years old, graying curly hair, wearing glasses through which you can clearly see his sad, his familial sad eyes. The most interesting detail, however, is about three or four inches from the advertising-gimmick picture frame; it represents (so unusual for these moderate continental climates) a standing Buddha, just awakened, stretching, i.e., in a state of total physical delight, with a protruding round and fleshy belly, which, some say, if gently stroked with the thumb, will make wishes come true. And all those sad eyes are looking at that Buddha as if they expect salvation, hope, illumination. Though from some other details contained in the room—for example, the mezuzah, the *hanukkiah,* a reproduction of Chagall's stained-glass window, a postcard from Hebron, the book *Tatsachen aus Israel 1968,* and other objects—we can conclude that the family framed in the cheap plastic frame is most likely to be of Jewish, I emphasize, *Jewish* extraction. What, then, is one standing Buddha of (let's say) cherry wood doing amid a foreign faith? Or what, for that matter—if you were bold enough to peer into the farthest corner—is the reproduction of El Greco's Jesus *(Salvador Mundi, Der Heilige Verlosser),* Savior of the World, doing carelessly leaning against the stereo speaker? But that goes beyond the limits of a description, it goes beyond the power with which a picture can speak, and therefore it is better to return, with a gentle swing back, to the desk, next to the Buddha, to the photographs we have seen, and then, through a familiar darkening, we completely vanish. We admit, fully, that we're not there.

Departure for the Spa.

Mother turned and took a last look at the room. Everything seemed to be all right, she said. Yes, Father turned, everything is all right. "You won't forget to water the flowers?" "We won't," said Father and I. "If you make tea now and then, feel free to toss the leftover tea into the ficus pot; it won't do it a bit of harm." "Don't worry," said Father. "Suzanna will come on Friday. Let her do the dusting, tidy up the room. If something special is needed, you tell her." "Everything is fine," said Father. "Don't worry." "You have enough cheese for two days," said Mother. "Great," I said. We stopped talking. Mother went back to the table, smoothed the lace tablecloth, and moved the crystal ashtray farther from the edge. "Better than that it should fall," she said. "Much better," we agreed. She looked around once more and sighed: "I could leave now." "We'll take you to the station," said Father. "Really," said Mother, "you needn't. I'll take the bus and . . . " "Nonsense," said Father. He took the travel bag, I took the suitcase. "Write to us." "I will," said Mother and started uncertainly toward the door. "Watch my house." "I am here," I said, "don't worry." "I'm not worrying," said Mother. "It's just . . . " "I understand," said Father, and we slammed the door behind us. "I hope you have nice weather." "That is what really matters," said Mother, "because if I have to sit for three weeks in some room . . . " "That would not be pleasant," said Father. "But still, the rest, the sleep, right?" "I'll write," said Mother. And immediately, almost silently, we hurried to wait for the bus. #46.

A Postcard. A Detail.

The postcard Mother sent us as soon as she arrived at the spa, sketched already in the roughest terms, contained one almost imperceptible detail, invisible, so to speak, to the naked eye. Only under the lens of a powerful stamp collector's magnifying glass did a minuscule black spot (seemingly, at first glance, an error in the manufacture of the postcard or the quality of the printer's ink) become what it truly was—a black bird in steady flight. On the two-dimensional surface of the photograph, it was located right above the warm-water baths, but in reality, when the professional photographer was leaning over his camera (no doubt affixed to a tripod), the black bird was much farther off, winging, no doubt, over nearby forests or meadows. Whatever the case—in reality, coincidentally—it did not manage to elude the cautious eye of the camera, thereby becoming, at least for me, a strange resolution to the most concealed of spiritual incompatibilities and physical passions, an exceptional and essential, unique *avis ex machina*. Coup de grâce. Tour de force. Everything.

Paying Attention to Father.

In short: At first everyone attributed it to my father's particular mood, to a solemn, festive intoxication, and then when the rooms filled with people, and he went on moving about, and then, even up to the moment when Father abruptly vanished in the direction of the bedroom and appeared, shortly thereafter, holding his daughter by her highly raised hand, only to deliver her over at once to the impatient groom, forgetting to request the obligatory recompense for a new bride, and even then—in the deliberate silence of their mutual glance, full of love, anxiety perhaps—when Father burst into a heaving, uncontrollable sob, convulsing like a man who has been taken ill suddenly on the street, only then, therefore, did the invited guests notice that he, my father, all that time had not been walking but rather hovering, or, more precisely, he was walking on air, a full six inches off the rug and the parquet floor, without touching bottom, without touching reality. But then, ah, *then* someone looked at the clock, time was mentioned, and the wedding party went racing down the stairs, down the main street, by Hotel Central, and onward, to the justice of the peace; and Father, alone in the empty apartment, stepped down off the invisible podium, stepping into empty space as if coming down off a high step, and perched on the edge of the nearest chair, engrossed in the cruel shrieks of the cuckoo from our wall clock, where he has remained sitting—though some have claimed to have seen him in the town hall building—to this very day: slightly reclining and pressing his left cheek, firmly, on his cracked, dry, vein-covered left palm.

The Return. Mother.

I don't know whether I'll be able to find the proper words. I lied to them about the joints, why not? I did recuperate some, put on some weight, but the joints, they will never get better, they'll kill me. I know that. I don't think about it. I look at them sometimes: my husband and my son. Should I talk about it? I came back from the spa, autumn came, I went out on the balcony. The leaves had fallen from the poplar; through the branches you could see much farther, farther than I'd expected. I don't see the mayor anymore—he must be feeling better now. They say that from time to time he laughs, but seldom, irregularly. The neighbor still spends the entire afternoon on his balcony; my stomach hurts, I feel naked when he peers through the window. At the spa I paid for two beds, only so I could be alone in my room. I like peace and quiet best. But my son has grown—he comes home later and later. Sometimes I'm not asleep, I wait to hear him. That's why I lied to them about my joints: they have their worries, they work. Why should I disturb them? Life is, after all, a burden that each person drags behind him. No one can help anyone else, no. Words of comfort? They haven't cured anybody yet, of this I'm certain. I have to clench my teeth and keep my silence, there. Some get by some other way? Presumably. But, next winter, I will be sixty-two. Ask me why I don't hope for anything anymore. How can I tell you? Perhaps it would be better if I asked you: what do you hope for? Or my husband? My son?

Conclusion.

Mother surprised us, we weren't expecting her. "How are you?" she said. "What have you been up to?" Father had been lying, half-asleep, on the sofa; I was filling out forms at the desk. "There," said Father, "there," but Mother paid no mind to his words. She stood calm, thrilled, before the kitchen door, her cheeks full, her hair light. I remembered her from my childhood, I tried to speak, but she closed the door behind her, walked over—you could hear her heels clicking on the concrete floor—to the stove, the refrigerator lonely in the corner, the shelves with dishes. Father said how she had put on some weight, looked much better, now, after the spa, but we did not get up. We stayed just like that. Stuck. Until she called us. To dinner.

■ □ ■ □ ■

THE PLAYGROUND

1

ON THE THIRTEENTH OF SEPTEMBER, 1972, ON OUR WAY BACK from our regular walk, Father and I discovered the playground. It is hard to believe that we'd never noticed it before: the oval concrete pavement, the labyrinths of iron bars, the sand. We turned off Primorska into Vuk Street, picking, unexpectedly, an obscure shortcut that ran to the main avenue of the city park. Here we caught sight of it through the thinning leaves: it beckoned to us, but we were afraid of the children, caught up in their games. We went on our way home there among the poplars and ash trees. Besides, we inadvertently caught sight of the time on the belfry of the Orthodox church: 6:22 P.M. Father muttered something about conflicts in the Near East as if he were apologizing, and immediately picked up the pace. "The TV news," I believe he said, "starts at 6:30." Above us, evening was cloaked in the red glow of sunset, the clouds were parading their perfection. I hurried to catch up with him. "Tonight," I told him, "tonight it's definitely not going to rain."

2

The day before, on Tuesday, Mother had come home from the Mataruška Health Spa. For the first time in three weeks

Father got up on time, he shaved, and, smelling of after-shave, he sat at the table, where the following things were waiting for him: a cup of herbal tea beneficial for the gall-bladder, a soft-boiled egg, a slice of bread, and two saccharin tablets. I listened to him cough in the bathroom and blow his nose, obviously delighted. He passed through the room on his tiptoes, sure that I was asleep, and came right back, groping for his forgotten eyeglasses in the green semidark of the lowered blinds. I opened my eyes and watched his back, bent in an anguished effort of teetering, as he passed through on his tiptoes and left the door nearly closed behind him, fearing the squeak of the door handle. Even in the kitchen his voice was soft, almost a whisper. Their faces appeared on the cloudy glass, but you couldn't hear the kiss. Father went out, Mother came in and cleaned the tiled stove, I got up, leaned my face on the windowpane: no one was coming. Only papers, filled-out forms, were piled neatly in the corner of the room. In a word: the day began.

3

Those years—Father was in his seventh, I in my third, and my mother in her sixth decade of life—we felt the need to cultivate a love for the unreliable season: autumn. During dinner Father said that autumn is the most like life itself. He felt that I should write something about this. Only a few sentences, he advised, compare autumn to people. Mention clarity and the clouds, a sky in which, as in the human mind, cloudy ideas clash, while the river, the bloodstream, trembles from restlessness and passion under the uncertain rays of the sun.

"Nonsense," said Mother. "Do you actually believe that I like this weather, first summer heat, then freezing rain?"

"I didn't say any such thing," answered Father, "I was talking about symbols. For me it is . . . "

"Tell me something," interrupted Mother. "How long will these joints of mine last? How much longer?"

Father stopped talking, he did not look up.

"Tell the truth, now," warned Mother.

"Well," said Father. "I'd rather not venture an opinion, it's not my department. How about we talk to a rheumatologist?"

"I want your opinion," said Mother.

Father took off his glasses, rubbed his eyes. "A dozen years," he said. He tried to smile.

"No more?"

"I guess."

Mother sighed, wiped her hands on her apron. She looked at me, at my plate; she placed the salt shaker in the middle of the table. "Would you like a little more soup?" she asked Father.

"Fine," he said, "but just half a ladle's worth."

"Half a ladle?" Mother said, surprised. She had already gotten up and gone to the stove, fingered the ladle, the pot lid.

"Fine," Father said suddenly.

"What?"

"I'll have a full bowl," he said. "Don't forget the noodles."

4

(Actually, this was a time when we, exhausted by debates about whether or not our earlier walks—now so vivid in my stories—had actually taken place, did begin taking walks, though, truth be told, they never had a preset route, some imagined path that included the center of town like the walks that existed in my manuscripts. Instead they described careless circles, routes chosen at random that had to fill only one condition: sooner or later they'd bring us home.)

5

We come up, serene, to the Holy Sepulchre, where divine silence is jarred by the blows of blacksmiths and carpenters. High up on scaffolding masons are moving about, and particles of dust grapple with the grains of light. A mumbling monk opens the little door of curving iron, we bend, Lucia kisses the stone of the pedestal. The monk's eyes are black, indifferent. In the prayer reaching us from his lips, I can see clearly, chisels and nails are pounding. When I take out a five-pound note, his *amen* swells; the candles flicker and hiss.

Jesus appears at noon. He is visibly pale, though wearing clean robes; his forehead is speckled with tiny, uneven scars; he is thin. He extends his arm, his thin hand touches Lucia's hair; it gleams, golden among his delicate fingers. Jesus leans over, kisses her forehead. That kiss is a little longer, and she closes her eyes the way she sometimes opens them for me. Her thighs quake, blood drains from her lips. Jesus raises two fingers and leaves, walking with the full length of his stride. Tourists and pilgrims press in, so he stops, strikes a pose. Under the glare of the flashes, his face takes on a ruddier hue.

Much later, while Lucia sits quiet on the stone bench, I light a candle for a friend. When he notices that I am crying, the priest blesses me and describes in the air, right above me, a cumbersome cross of olive wood. I make it to the door, I stagger, I leave it by the door. Outdoors, in the daylight, all crosses are heavier to bear.

We are not far from the Wailing Wall.

5a

"All of that is a dream," says Father, "it's all a dream."

At Radecki we stop, we turn around. No one is following us. Only the boats are moving.

6

A few days after my sister's wedding, Mother began talking to things. I don't know how we figured it out (who saw her first?); in any case, the house had been deserted for a few weeks. On the tables and in the corners of the room, unnatural quantities of carnations and yellow roses were wilting. We made a heap of the ribbons and sheets outside the balcony door in expectation of winter. Then photographs began to come: cold, rigid, vain in their attempt at capturing the atmosphere, the love. From time to time my sister's crooked teeth would show, or the groom's balding head. He, Stjepan, was a communist, a Catholic, an electrical engineer, living on a scholarship from the Niš television factory. They rented an apartment in our building, and at first we never saw them. Later their visits became more frequent and lasted longer: for hours all of us would sit and stare at the television screen. "Where is the love?" Mother would fret. "In my day . . ."

"Hush," said Father, "each of us learns in his own way." And he stayed dressed only in his undershirt and poplin boxer shorts, too capacious for his skinny, scraggly legs that ended in unexpected children's feet. Size 39.

7

That is how our real walks began. No one was positive anymore whether we had taken walks earlier, in the past. "What is the past, anyway?" asked Mother whenever the discussions began. Father brandished his war diary with excitement. He pulled out back issues of *Antword-Postkarten,* the whole *Kriegsgefangenenpost.* "That is history," answered Mother, "that doesn't prove a thing."

"This is a tragedy," countered Father, "the passage of time."

"Everything in its season," Ruben Rubenović, former

textiles salesman, soothed them. We still hadn't gotten used to the permanence of my sister's departure, so we embraced his visits with unconcealed gratitude. "To every thing there is a season: war and peace, tears and merriment, memory and oblivion." He had white hair, heavy eyelids, a loose lower lip.

"Tell her," Father addressed him, "explain to her, please."

"Don't talk about what came before," said Ruben Rubenović, "because there is nothing new under the sun. What came before will come again."

"Exactly," said Mother and applauded.

"Whose side are you on?" Father asked him.

"The heart is half a prophet," smiled the salesman and raised an index finger. "I do not deny your yesterday—it is real, just as your today is real, which is your future."

"There you have it," Father spoke to Mother.

"Tomorrow is a secret," I said to myself.

"The book of Prophets . . . ," began Ruben Rubenović.

"A priori I disagree," Father dismissed this with the flick of a hand.

"You are such a strange man," Mother said, surprised.

In Ruben Rubenović's sad eyes a smile hovered: "Everybody gets the same in the end," he said.

"We were talking about the reality of our earlier walks," Father said with irritation. "What connection can there be between one's doubts in the veracity of some event and the biblical book of Prophets?"

"Because every work will come before a judge and every secret shall be confessed."

Father stared at Ruben Rubenović. He thought to speak, but didn't, instead twisting his lips.

"So?" asked Mother.

"We didn't take those walks," confessed Father.

"What about his stories?"

"His stories? Whose?"

"To be frank," said the old merchant, "now that I think of it, I used to run into you on the river shore and by the cemetery. The boy was just beginning to grow. I remember how gangly he was by your side."

"I wore his olive-green jacket," I said.

"From Italy," Father choked.

Mother looked at us, surprised. "So you took those walks, after all?"

We didn't answer. Ruben Rubenović begged our pardon, said he had to be going, and reached for his black hat with the wide rim. Father shook hands with him awkwardly, Mother did the same; he patted me on the head with his dry, narrow hand. His coat was worn, the inside gleamed white along the edges of the deep pockets. He stopped at the door, tall, hunched. "We used to talk about wisdom," he said, "and I completely forgot to tell you this." He coughed, moved the cane from one hand to the other.

"The heart, among the wise, is on the right side."

8

We needed more than three weeks to decide. First we conducted all possible research. We measured time, space, paths, frequency of arrivals. We noted the lovers who, under the starry sky, climbed to the very tip of the rocketship of metal bars. We noticed the beggar who was dozing every morning on a swing. The squirrels scampering about on the oval concrete pavement didn't bother us either. And so it was that we arrived, on October fifth, at 11:15 P.M. I fashioned an awkward castle in the sand; Father crept through the rectangular labyrinth. We spent ten minutes together above the world on the elevated wooden platform. Father was on the swing for a while, and then we approached the seesaw. In the pale moonlight, the church belfry showed 11:42 P.M. I am no longer certain who was the first to speed up the rhythm of pushing off. Sometimes in my sleep there is a pang of pain in my thighs from the strength of the push; other times I see my father's red face, I hear his loud shout, the eyeglasses slipping from his crooked nose. He separates from the other end of the seesaw and slowly, raising his arms and flinging back his head, he takes off into the night, into the cosmos. I run, I breathe, I wake up—I find myself racing wildly through the Zemun streets while my father halts, descends to the moon like some powerful machine, and lies down at once, drops off to sleep. At the bottom of the concrete pedestal, the broken glass of his spectacles (nearsighted) reflects a more unusual image of the world, where, without order or purpose, natural and artificial catastrophes follow one upon another: earthquakes, currency devaluations, wars, and old age, which we have never managed to confront. By then my father had managed to find another "Ghetaldus," another tortoiseshell frame, and he stands there, not lonely but separate, in the middle of the main street. As the lens of the camera moves back faster and faster, scanning the rows of renovated houses on both sides of the street, he vanishes, sinking into the bustle of the eternal, losing himself under massive letters as unambiguous as their black color:

THE END

9

But this is not, in fact, the real end: quite the contrary. We are faced with an abundance of completely new images; we are filled with the halftones of unwritten music. We give ourselves, with an unclear smile, to the dying touch of a flood of associations. We harken to time.

For the paths of escape are many and they are poorly explored.

Like that sentence of Lucia's, uttered between rows of linden trees, before which all constraints, all zones of hampered movement vanished and unexplored realms beckoned, undulating worlds, dimensions of dimensions.

"I feel claustrophobia on Earth," said Lucia.

And we lay on our backs. In the grass. To look at the stars.

■ □ ■ □ ■

THE DAMP

FIRST AUTUMN. THEN THE DAYS GREW LONG LIKE LEAP YEARS, ripe and damp. Father was puzzled: Mother claimed that the "newly built high-rises," across from our building and near the river, "obstructed the access of fresh air." She apparently thought that fresh air is necessary, that "winds of change" are key. But Father simply posed the question. "I don't get it," he said. "What about all the other seasons? Winter, for instance." Well, there wasn't much to say about winter; it was brief and mild. Then the spring. The spring, I'm sure, we remembered for the hyacinths, the countless hyacinths. Father kept insisting on the natural fact that spring and fall are transitional seasons. "Transitional!" he would exclaim and raise his finger. "Which means," he continued, "that they have to include the basic features of the seasons they connect: winter and summer." Then he peered at us. "Have I made myself clear?" he asked. But spring. Spring isn't like anything: it has no flavor, no fragrance, no will of its own, it is bland, slimy to the touch. Fall: now that's something else again. Everything was tangible, everything unfolded according to old church calendars, according to the chronologies at the Jewish Community Center in Split. Father was gradually easing his way into retirement. We advised him to have others cover for him, to avoid extra shifts at the hospital, but he refused. In those days, salaries were shooting up dramatically at his hospital, and doctors were fighting to be assigned extra loads; it all had to do with the number of years they'd worked, average income, that sort of thing. Mother followed the reports from the Council on Retirement in Vrnjačka Banja. A fierce debate was raging on how far back to take the average when calculating pension payments; there were quandaries, complaints, the Republic's representatives held conflicting views. When the radio announced the decision to calculate pensions on the basis of the average salary over the last ten years, Father requested that they boost his number of night shifts. It seemed to us that he was never home at all, that day and night he was birthing, performing abortions, conducting complex gynecological procedures. Sometimes we found bloodstains on the cuffs of his pants. "Oh," Father would say, "that—a Caesarean, an unforgettably narrow cervical passage, no other way to save the mother's life." "The child?" we'd ask. "Yes, well, the child . . . " Then the first grapes appeared, perhaps still unripe, but large, translucent. Mother strained them, first for Rosh Hashanah, then for Yom Kippur, and poured the new wine into glasses we would use that one time and never again. We prepared the ritual New Year's meal in the kitchen. Father stayed longer at the temple, but came back in high spirits. "Lord," he said, "what a crowd was there. I've never seen so many people. I don't know what that signifies." Now we know. Then we didn't, but now we do: while Father wondered, Mother claimed that "what we have here is overpopulation, crowded living conditions," that "with these newfangled buildings" they have simply cut us off from the world, from the river. "The river is the life source," says Mother and falls silent. "The Danube?" asks Father. "Every river," says Mother, "there is no difference between the Danube and the Nile." "Or the Amazon," says Father, "as vast as a sea." These are the sorts of conversations we have. What else can we do? The days are endless, as long (I think I've said this before) as years. Mornings are hot, evenings don't bring hoped-for freshness, beds are hot and lumpy, there are mosquitoes, there are all kinds of bugs, more and more wasps, bats. The sun stands like this in the sky: a simple, searing ball against the white backdrop of eternity. "Sounds too poetic for my taste," says Father. We don't know what we are talking about anymore. We go off for a walk in the early evening, about six; Father takes his umbrella. "Such dampness," says Mother, "and no rain." She feels an explanation must be sought in "sudden barometric pressure changes" and in "atmospheric pollution." "Atomic explosions," she says, "have destabilized certain fundamental relations in nature. It used to be that you could know precisely how much of this and how much of that existed in the world around us. After all, the animal species never were tempted by self-destruction, but today?" She feels that the "great powers-that-be" are responsible for it all. Father says, "I don't know." We halt in front of the former Yugoslav Air Force base. Two men in white are playing tennis; a little farther away soldiers are playing soccer. "Perhaps it is best that way," says Father. "Do you see the sweat on their backs?" I nod. "Everything exudes in that sweat," he says, "all the filth of the human body." We start a conversation about the filth of the human soul, but quickly stop speaking. "Perhaps it would be more comfortable if we sat on a bench," I suggest, but Father declines. He fears his pants will stick to his body; sweat is corroding his skin, he says. I remind him of what he has just said; I point out the obvious divergence of the two statements. "It should be washed off immediately," he concludes, "or otherwise . . . " "No," says Mother when we return, "I have no particular views on sweat." We eat supper in silence (cheese, café au lait, yogurt, leftover meat patties, honey), then we open all the windows, turn off the lights, turn on the television. Cautiously, like an indecisive creature, the damp enters the room, adheres to the walls, settles on the floor, touches our hands, faces, eyebrows, devours us, but we are powerless, or, no, we are not powerless, we simply do not resist, what is the point of resisting? We sit, we watch, the announcer says something but we don't know what, the television speakers have been broken for some time, we watch only the image. "Excuse me?" says Mother. Father is of the opinion that the previous picture was of Berlin; Mother believes that it was Stockholm, or perhaps Oslo, but by no means Berlin. "By no means Berlin," she says. Father is obstinate. "Berlin," he says, then tips back his cup of kefir, closes his eyes, the white fluid drips, with the damp, down his throat. There are some words we gave up on utterly some time back: transience, inevitability, death. Death we dare mention only in prayers, like last autumn for the High Holidays. It couldn't be helped. Father and I stood with our yarmulkes on; he read, recalling, with effort, certain words, and the amazing, guttural language, enhanced by his raspy, half-sobbing voice, filled the kitchen. There hadn't been any damp then. It was autumn, early autumn, Mother had made a pumpkin pie, first for New Year's, then when I asked her to. And now, a year (sixteen months?) after the guarantee was up, which had been issued by the construction company that built our apartment, plaster and oil-based paint were peeling off the walls in large strips. Mother cleaned, but stains remained on the parquet floor, big white splotches that required steel wool or a razor to really clean them. We called the Municipal Housing Authority, but as far as they were concerned, these were unfavorable climatic conditions. We would have to bide our time until the weather improved; if we went ahead and did the work now, within a few days the exact same thing would happen again. "Do you claim that the damp is to be blamed for everything?" Father asked. "Hard to say, Comrade," they answered him, "but . . . " "Should we get back in touch with you later," asked Father, "in a few weeks' time, perhaps?" "You may," they said, "though we are keeping a file on this, don't worry." "Just to check," said Father. "Just to check, you can call," they said. Someone chuckled at the other end of the line. "Good-bye," hollered Father, raising his voice. "All our best," they answered.

Father hung up. "Will they come?" asked Mother. "They won't," said Father. "They aren't doing anything because of all this dampness." Mother nodded, went to the window. Outside visibility was limited, shortened to a few meters. The new buildings could only barely be seen, the river was out of sight. When you step out of a building you can feel exactly how the damp presses down on you, how it doesn't allow you to move freely; you have to shove your way through, to walk with your shoulder leaning into the damp to push through more easily. Men resemble icebreakers. Women are completely lost. The damp warps their faces, their makeup, strands of hair dangle down their necks, down their shoulders, no matter what they do to straighten it it curls, tangles, dresses don't flutter, they stick to the thighs, moist rubber presses into flesh. But when the weather is like this I fall in love. These things generally don't last long, but the feeling is powerful and full, and helps me, for at least a few days, to forget the damp. She stands at the entrance to the garden. She is dressed in a light nylon T-shirt and a plaid, slightly outmoded skirt. With the fingers of her left hand, she touches her wide wedding band, which, because of the humidity, has no gleam. I cross the street slowly, step by step, trying to make her notice me, see me. Here, probably because of the many gardens, the damp is thinner, there is less of it, one breathes more easily. I stand right next to her: over her shoulder I see garlands of garlic; I see kale, cucumbers; there are flowers, a pear tree. I think how pretty she is and how large—how large, pretty, and strong this woman is! Suddenly she speaks to me: "My husband is gravely ill," she says. The next day I come back again, I keep watch, I stroll along the fence. From deep inside the garden appears a man, he comes over to the garden gate, he leans on it, he rests his cheek on his hand, he watches me. Is this her husband? I walk quickly away, and only when I reenter the thicker sediment of dampness do I turn again. I don't see him, but his eyes follow me, I feel that they follow me, that even when he closes his yellowed eyelids he is following me, and I am forced to run, to run to the riverside, where, out of breath, I greedily breathe in the fresh air and almost choke on the huge amounts of moisture in it. Changing clothes is also agonizing. When we come back from our walks, we simply yank off our wet, sticky clothes, like some vast larvae; we are ashamed, but we have no strength to show our own shame. The advantage of our apartment, we always used to say, is the fact that it lies between light and shadow: while some of the rooms are warm and full of sunshine, the others are pleasantly cool with a greenish gloom, silence. Here we drink our afternoon coffee. But now, Mother claims, everything has changed, "since our park was destroyed" and "the poplar trees were cut down on the next street over." Father spreads his arms in a shrug. His gestures recently have become lighter (he would say more moderate), they take longer. He used to be capable of shrugging more quickly than the time it takes for a blow to hit a gong, but now he spreads his arms slowly, for hours, even days. The trouble is that time and weather have merged; we can no longer distinguish them. The damp is probably getting into clockworks, springs, probably slowing down the hands. It is hard to say what is time and what weather—all of it is nature, everything constantly repeats, there is no end, no beginning, no distinctions. Only Mother, thanks to her hidden instincts, finds the right time for each meal; she is never late. At noon, or later, Father sounds the agreed-on family signal: two short and one long ring. Someone opens the door for him, he comes in, the soup is steaming on the table—dinner. The bread is damp. We don't say anything. It seems to me that we haven't been speaking for ages, but am I wrong? I feel sure that last fall we used to talk quite often. Mother was straining the big grapes, and Father and I, handing each other glasses of the sour-sweet liquid, discussed all manner of things: politics, the soccer championship, potential war zones, on-duty work at the clinic, the number of miscarriages, new books. It was autumn. Together we went to the movies. One evening we set out for the theater, but for whatever reason, I don't know why, we gave up and returned, along the quay, homeward. Then the days became inhumanly long. Time merged with weather, the damp destroyed everything, we could only measure ourselves by it. Several times, during a walk, it would seduce us, drive us to take a wrong turn, to walk in circles. We found ourselves, I remember it well, right at the water's edge; the river gurgled maliciously and rose, splashing our feet, hoping to grab us. We even considered not going out anymore, but they overpowered us, those walks, those departures, those meanders along the same paths; there was no way to avoid them, or did we even try? At that time, Father was tending toward immortality. Mother, of course, cast all the blame "on the damp," on "unbearable living conditions" that hadn't "changed a whit for months" and showed not even a "whisper of improvement." Yes, that is how it was, I don't deny it. At night you couldn't even see the stars; you couldn't see anything. You moved around in a perfect armor of dampness, like an embryo in some vast womb of weather. We looked, but we couldn't see. Our eyes were open, but our gaze didn't reach anywhere, anything. Only the damp, that was all. Only the damp. I felt Father near me by instinct. I think I knew that I would touch him if I stretched out my hand, that he was there next to me, that he was walking at the same pace, that he was not moving farther from me. Father later told me that he felt the same way. The difference was only in his desire, beyond the knowledge that I was there, to touch me, to confirm his knowledge of my proximity, to defeat some deep-seated doubt that man is alone in the world. The tendency to immortality included vitamin B-15, Caucassian kefir, Gerovitol, fresh cheese, and salves that Father eagerly rubbed into his skin, standing completely naked in the bathroom after a bath. But despite it all, his face got longer, slipped downward, the bags under his eyes did not disappear even after a good night's sleep, and the two sharp creases, running from his nose to the corners of his mouth, grew even deeper. The longing for departure, for change, was normal. It erupted immediately, in all of us. We thought that it would be good to go off somewhere, maybe to the sea or the mountains, just to get away, to separate the climatic pace from the temporal variety. You can imagine how the damp affected Mother's joints. "There were nights," she said, "when even closing my eyelids was an awful trial, pain I couldn't bear." And the beds. A person had the feeling he was lying on a damp, sandy beach, the moisture mixing with sweat, the sweat soaking into the bedclothes; there was no point in taking baths: terry cloth abraded the skin, clean clothes stuck to the body and between the legs, talcum powder—shaken on the chafed spots—turned into an extra layer of skin, into scales, shoes cracked at the seams, stockings tore, freshly ironed trousers wrinkled and stretched at the knees, cuffs on shirts frayed, the knots on ties turned into choking nooses, the handkerchief for wiping my forehead couldn't be washed clean, soapsuds wouldn't wash hands clean, fingers stuck to each other, it took superhuman effort to peal index finger from middle finger, to pluck the thumb from a fist, sweat gnawed at belts and waistbands, wristwatches dropped with a bang to the floor, ice melted in the refrigerator, the water in hot water heaters seethed, combs broke off large locks of hair, mirrors were coated with a thin layer of dense droplets, keyholes—blackened and rusty—resisted keys. The days—now I can say this with certainty—were longer than twenty-four hours. Something was hovering in the air, a natural disaster was engraving its name into the events around us. The sun stood in the sky like this: a meaningless, searing ball that wouldn't budge from its place for any price. Tragedy. Every day we expected tragedy. In the evening we'd lie down in bed as soon as we'd said good-night, uncertain of whether we'd be seeing or recognizing each other in the morning.

That is how it was. Mother felt that "last year's record attendance" at the temple was actually, when she thought about it now, a reflection of "misconstrued presentiments," that people were drawn to that last gathering "by something from within." She didn't believe that this was a "rebirth of faith." "To my mind," she said, "nature is orgasming." "Antimatter," said Father, "destroys matter." There is no time, there is no climate, there is no history, everything is nothing, nothing is everything, everything repeats, there is no beginning, no end, observations are deceptive, illusions frequent, the truth has lost its meaning. Perhaps more should be added: that every event has before it an unlimited selection of possibilities and that comparisons are untenable. Therefore, the final scenes of this play are observed, I emphasize, (first) from the window and (second) through a slightly open door. Do these conditions bring their truthfulness into question? For everything began with Father's shout. Mother and I ran into the room. Father was standing by an open window, in front of the bulk of the dampness, and hurriedly waving his arms. We came closer. "Look," he said, and pointed up high, toward the tops of the new high-rises. And we could see how the damp was vanishing, disappearing, disappearing into itself, sinking down further and further. Presently we caught sight—for the first time in a long time!—of the houses across the way, then the riverbanks, the river, the capital city in the distance. It looked as if nothing had changed. By then the damp had sunk to the bottom, touched the pavement, the grass, and the sidewalk, and started to break up, dissolve into largish and then smaller and smaller chunks. Then it was gone. Sometimes, on another street, we'd catch sight of a leftover swirl, but it didn't last long. By the next day we already could have begun doubting whether the damp had been there at all, but we didn't. From the place where we were, from the window of our second-floor apartment, we became witnesses to a sunny, meaningless, pure day. Nothing had changed, we could have said. What *hadn't* changed?

asked Mother instead. Two or three days later, Father got one of his regular gallbladder attacks and was taken, that same afternoon, to the city hospital. The damp had completely worn him down, said Mother. The hospital aides lifted him up and carried him down the stairs. A floor below, his moaning suddenly ceased, he abruptly shrank, went limp, his head flopped onto the shoulder in the white coat, spittle dribbled from the corner of his mouth. Now all of us could see that he was crying—the on-call doctor, the hospital aides, neighbors, some children, garbage collectors, the traffic cop—and he looked at me through his crooked glasses, at how I was peeking out through the partly open door while his artificial teeth were banging against the taut skin of his cheek, and the yellowed hands remained behind him even when they had gone quite far off. Then they came to repair our apartment. Mother chose the colors, the rooms filled with an entirely new light, and we put tiles in the bathroom and tiled the bathtub. On Wednesday I told her that I might go off, again, on some sort of trip. She went over to the window. Outside the branches were swinging in gentle gusts of wind, the leaves, at the top, were yellow. "I knew it," she said. "Pardon?" I asked. And she answered: "It's autumn again."

■ □ ■ □ ■

THE GREAT REBELLION AT THE STULN NAZI CAMP

1. My father's hair turned gray on March 18, 1961.

2. Two large, clear teardrops welled in his eyes.

3. "Not from unexpected self-pity," he protested later, "but because of the change. A change which demanded that I understand time, that I notice its passage and admit to its implacability. That I obey it more diligently."

4. Until then, therefore, my father did not acknowledge the implacability of time or its necessity.

5. In this, my father was similar to the heroes of antiquity.

6. Or were the heroes of antiquity aware of time after all?

7. (Did the heroes of antiquity fully possess their own timelessness? Their out-of-time-ness?)

8. Unlike the heroes of antiquity, my father often, before and after the stated date, in conversation or during his afternoon monologues, compared time with money. "Time is like money," my father would say. "The older it is, the more it's worth. The rarer it is, the more significant."

9. My father, as an amateur of course, dabbled in numismatics. He had over four hundred different coins. He had no idea what at least half of them represented.

10. He had about fifty monetary bills, mostly from the Independent State of Croatia and prewar Yugoslavia.

11. It is crucial to state that my father developed and per-

fected a longish list of terms and concepts closely aligned to his favorite topic of conversation: Time and Money. Unfortunately, it is impossible in this limited space to even list them, let alone go into any detailed description. But from the initial logical postulate, i.e., that time is money, it is obvious that for every situation known to the monetary and the financial world, my father had a corresponding temporal counterpart (and vice versa).

12. Inflation of time, for instance.

13. Or the time market. A dropping time rate. The second-world dollar. The middle ages of money. A deficit of time. A temporal crisis.

14. Revaluation of time as well.

15. His favorite term, however, was "mechanical time." He maintained that with the industrial production of watches, alarm clocks, even church towers, time had gotten nothing. Quite the contrary, it could only lose. The fact that time is always within reach, claimed my father, only creates an irreparable multidimensionality and distortion of real Time. That and nothing more. And since, fortunately, "mechanical time" is based on the principle of the spring, a product of a given technological process, and technology has no place in determining Time, my father simply did not acknowledge any mechanical and electronic manipulation when calculating Time. Without blinking, of course, he was happy to accept any hourglass or, in his opinion, the most ideal of all: sundials in gardens and on the walls of houses.

16. He was most indifferent to atomic timepieces.

17. What happened, meanwhile, to the heroes of antiquity?

18. The heroes of antiquity would disappear the moment they grasped the transitory nature of time.

19. Here is one more difference between the heroes of antiquity and my father: my father, on March 19, 1961, understood Time, but he did not disappear.

20. Quite the contrary. His overall physical condition improved visibly.

21. But, alas! The consequences of his participation in the Second World War were indelible.

22. In the year 1941, in the spring, my father—as the reserve sanitation officer in the Royal Yugoslav Army—was wading up to his knees in the Timok River, but his heroism only reached its fullest after blowing up the Bor Copper Mine.

23. The military command issued the following decree: "We are retreating, but we will not leave anything for the enemy! In the name of the king and our fatherland!"

24. They laid out explosives up in the Bor Copper Mine.

25. BOOM!!!

26. The Bor Copper Mine blew up. (The enemy was advancing on all sides.)

27. My father—a young reserve sanitation officer of the Royal Yugoslav Army in collapse—was present at that act in an unusually vital capacity. He was in charge of caring for anyone injured during the blast.

28. Indeed, my father vividly recalls, rocks spewed up to 320 meters from the mine entrance.

29. It is believed, however, that there were rocks which hurtled even farther.

30. A soldier, jerking back at the moment of the blast, injured his finger, which was hooked into his gun belt buckle.

31. The bang was enormous.

32. Horses neighed.

33. The Bor Copper Mine ceased to exist.

34. My father was of the opinion that the soldier's finger should be amputated. He proposed total anesthesia and ordered that all the instruments be boiled.

35. Then a medic noticed that the soldier had, in his opinion, merely sprained his finger.

36. The soldier was sitting on a tree stump, smoking.

37. My father said that he would only know for certain once the patient was on the table. Until then, he stressed,

the outcome was entirely unknown. The enemy was advancing on all sides, and every pair of hands was needed. If he were to hesitate, my father thought, human loss would be inevitable.

38. My father went into the tent.

39. The medic went over to the soldier, and with a few deft movements he returned the injured joint to its place.

40. The soldier thanked him. He said that it hurt much less, but he would like to know how much longer the finger would be this swollen.

41. The medic said that it would last a day or two. He washed the hand and went off with the cured soldier to eat.

42. The afternoon bugles sounded.

43. At that moment my father came out of the tent all in white, with a surgical apron around his waist and warm surgical gloves on his hands.

44. In front of the sanitation tent there was nobody at all.

45. The soldier's cigarette butt was distinctly visible in the green grass.

46. As a well-trained reserve officer of the Royal Yugoslav Army and an exemplary student of the Zagreb University School of Medicine, my father stood, so to speak, at attention, waiting for events to take their course.

47. Two weeks later, at dawn, the entire regiment surrendered to the Germans. A certain number of soldiers were executed on the spot.

48. The enemy had been quite far from the site of the explosion at the time the Bor Copper Mine was blown up. When the enemy saw the destroyed equipment, the enemy was quite surprised.

49. Some German officers, my father recalls vividly, were extremely angry. They raged and howled out curt, harsh sentences in German.

50. All the German officers shouted in German.

51. The translator asked: "Where are the French engineers

who were in charge of exploiting the Bor Copper Mine?"

52. The answer was: "The French engineers who were in charge of exploiting the Bor Copper Mine ran away."

53. The translator translated this response into German.

54. *"Was?"* said one German officer. He was wearing glasses.

55. Then the translator asked: "Did the French engineers participate in blowing up the Bor Copper Mine?"

56. "Yes, they did," was the answer.

57. The translator translated the response into German.

58. *"Was?"* said a second German officer. He was not wearing glasses.

59. The first German officer didn't say anything.

60. And so it was that my father and his entire regiment became prisoners of war of the Vermacht. On slow trains, through the Vojvodina, Croatia, and Austria, they were transported to officers' and other camps throughout Germany. Soldiers and officers, ordinary troops and colonels, they stood by the little windows and bade farewell to their native land. Some of them cried. Some were unshaven. A choking smell rose from the corners of the wagon.

61. Lübeck.

62. Nürnberg.

63. Stuln.

64. Four years later, in late winter, my father returned home. He was wearing an American sweater and American pants and an American shirt and American shoes. On his head he had an old hat, dusky in color, which came to his ears and slid down his forehead. In his right hand he held a peeling army box in which he had a shaving kit and 712 letters and postcards, *correspondance des prisonniers de guerre.*

65. At the time my father was not my father.

66. All in all, and in comparison with some other officers, prisoners of war, my father had exceptionally poor luck—he gained only four pounds.

67. There were Englishmen, my father vividly recalls,

who had to let out the seams on their trousers monthly. Or they walked around on green meadows, constantly patting their bellies.

68. (History soon showed whose suffering was worth more: my father's or that of the Englishmen who patted themselves on the belly.)

69. The English ate chocolate every day, my father went on to recall vividly. Maybe that is what influenced the inevitable loosening of their stomach muscles?

70. In any case, this was quite a nasty picture: all those Englishmen, officers, mostly soldiers, with sagging bellies, who were no longer able to snap to salute sharply at the command "Attention!"

71. Quite a nasty picture.

72. The Germans also ate chocolate every day, but they were so slender, so upright.

73. How their heels clicked!

74. My father was the first to suspect that girdles might be playing a key role in the German case.

75. "During a group outing," my father vividly recalls, "in the immediate vicinity of the camp, I spotted a textiles factory."

76 What could a textiles factory in the immediate proximity of a German camp for imprisoned officers in the heart of Nazi Germany be producing?

77. "Girdles," said my father.

78. "Girdles," concurred several Polish prisoners.

79. English officers held a two-day hunger strike. They demanded emergency approval for the use of girdles among the prisoners.

80. The German command ordered that three Yugoslav and seven Russian majors be shot summarily.

81. So that is how the great rebellion in the Nazi camp in Stuln was repressed.

82. The Stuln Nazi Camp was an international camp, which the Americans liberated shortly before the end of the war.

83. This explains why my father returned dressed in an American sweater and American pants and an American shirt and American shoes.

84. This, of course, does not explain why my father came home wearing the old hat, dusky in color, which reached his ears and slid down his forehead.

85. The old hat dusky in color is another story.

86. My father has never told me that story.

87. The hat sits, even today, in the closet. Mother says sometimes that the time has come to get rid of all unpleasant mementos. She suggests that we throw out the hat. Or, better yet, give it to the Red Cross.

88. "What use can the Red Cross have for one old hat, dusky in color, which I have had since the Second World War?" asks my father. "The Red Cross is a humane, massive organization that collects tens of thousands of blankets and tents, and sends them to Nicaragua, Guatemala, Palestine, Pakistan . . . wherever they are needed."

89. "Thank God we don't need anything," says Mother.

90. So the hat stays in the closet. It smells of lavender and tobacco leaves, which Mother slips into closed places against moths. Now and then, however, and particularly on March 18, 1961—when his hair first turned gray—my father takes it from the closet, and with the hat on his head, he stands in front of the mirror.

91. Two big, clear tears welled, then, in his eyes

92. He slowly took off the hat and ran trembling fingers through his white hair.

93. The streets at that moment were full of evening strollers.

94. There is no chronicle that records the heroic role my father played in blowing up the Bor Copper Mine.

95. (After the Second World War, with the transition to national ownership, the renovated Bor Copper Mine suddenly began to flourish. In 1958, it produced 2,268,000 tons of copper ore.)

96. But there are chronicles that record less valiant roles of heroes even less significant than my father. These are what we call "subjective chronicles."

97. In my father's opinion, "objective history" does not yet exist. An awareness of the historical role of individuals makes the existence of "objective history" impossible.

98. "In a certain way," my father admits, "I, too, am one of those individuals. I obstruct history."

99. At that moment, two big, clear teardrops welled in the eyes of my father. He left the hat in its place, went into the living room, and switched on the television.

100. Cowboys and fearless champions of law and order flitted across the screen.

101. My father cried long into the night.

■ □ ■ □ ■

THE MOVIES

The Man Who Shot Liberty Valance

THE MAN WHO SHOT LIBERTY VALANCE IS STANDING AT OUR front door. Mother can't make up her mind. "Should I let him in?" she asks. "What should I say?" The Man Who Shot Liberty Valance is wearing civilian clothing, but clothing does not influence one's character, clothing does not make the man, not a man like The Man Who Shot Liberty Valance. I shrug. "No." Father is clear, firm. "I doubt," he says, "sudden changes of human nature, unforeseeable changes because of *causa finalis,* especially changes in traits buried in our genes, in the RNA and DNA molecules. Can a man who has killed," he asks, "stop killing?" "You heard?" says Mother. The Man Who Shot Liberty Valance is putting his black valise down in front of our threshold. "I heard," he says. "With two votes against and one withheld," Mother says, "you will remain outside the door." "Anything you say," says The Man Who Shot Liberty Valance, "anything you say." Mother closes the door, hooks the chain. Outdoors streetlamps are lit, stars are lit, the moon is lit, rockets are lit, everything is lit, the whole city is in flames. I peek through an imaginary peephole in the door: The Man Who Shot Liberty Valance is rolling a cigarette. Crumbs of tobacco are fluttering down. They fall next to a crumpled sheet of cigarette paper. "What is he doing?" Mother asks me. "He's waiting," I say. "Waiting?" "Waiting." "Waiting?" asks Father.

"Yes," I say. "Let him wait," says Father. And Mother: "Let him wait." "Let him wait," I say.

. . .

"The Man Who Shot Liberty Valance," says Father, "ha-ha! Ha-ha-ha! Consciousness, my son, consciousness! Hmmmm! Fictional characters do not come to life. You listen here: experience is talking, age, years spent in work and the struggle for survival, shifts at the hospital, sleepless nights, Caesarean sections, miscarriages, hands that must never tremble, aching eyes, hair growing implacably white and getting thinner and thinner at the back. Why don't you listen to me for once? Reality is all there is, the whiteness of this day and the blackness of night, morning, noon. No, that is time, time doesn't exist, but day and night, fog, a stream, weeping willows. That is all, son; except for that, nothing exists, nothing is tangible, visible. But maybe I have set out on the wrong road, maybe I should reexamine myself? Maybe old age should get lost in fruitless games of the imagination, in wanderings through forests of lollipops, through paradisiacal gardens, through glass mountains? Maybe the mistake is in the fundamental position, in rejection. But, listen to me, wisdom is speaking to you, experience, age! Even if you choose that other side, the side invisible, absent, inaccessible to the senses, even if you do that, what will you accomplish? You'll call it reality. You'll call it reality, and it will end up the same. The game is, therefore, identical; it is not important which side you start playing from. The unreal continues to exist beyond the reach of the brain."

. . .

One of Spinoza's thoughts: "He who would distinguish the true from the false must have an adequate idea of what is true and what is false."

. . .

What do we see in the character of The Man Who Shot Liberty Valance?

A handsome figure.

A universal symbol of man.

Reception of the classic theory of the superiority of the male sex.

Confirmation of the slogan: sound mind in sound body.

Affirmation of physical education as essential to building the spiritual side of man's spirit.

A trimly tailored black velvet vest.

A rather decadent orientation toward the manufacturing form of production.

A return to old fashion: the symbol of people's everlasting dissatisfaction.

A return of pomade.

A trimmed mustache.

An easygoing, relaxed attitude.

A pensive look, achieved by mildly knitting the eyebrows while at the same time raising the right or left eyebrow.

Pipe tobacco as a concrete response to the increasingly poor production of cigarettes, or rather, as a concrete response to *planned* competition, which is only reflected in poor quality and constantly raising prices.

In that sense, according to this last definition, The Man Who Shot Liberty Valance stands on the side of the powerless consumer.

. . .

When Mother opens the door, The Man Who Shot Liberty Valance takes off his hat and, with a deep bow, takes her shopping basket and net bag. Mother goes, turning with a brittle smile, into the grocery store. The Man Who Shot Liberty Valance goes down the steps behind her, but out on the street, in front of the shop, he catches up with her in two or three strides and opens the door. "Thank you," says Mother. "You're welcome," says The Man Who Shot Liberty

Valance. "One mineral water," says Mother, "two cartons of milk, two bottles of peach juice, a loaf of bread, laundry soap, toothpaste, toilet paper." The Man Who Shot Liberty Valance goes over to the crates of bottles, stands on tiptoe. "Three Hearts mineral water?" he asks. "Oh," Mother turns. "No, no! Prince Miloš, please," she says.

. . .

Things that never happened with The Man Who Shot Liberty Valance:

An excursion to the outskirts of the city.

A stroll through Zemun, across the quay, by Venice to Šaran, perhaps even beyond, and back: across the outdoor market, through the main street and city park, to the fire station and the Third Business High School, along October 22nd Street home.

A long conversation on morals, law, order, violence.

A group photograph.

An entry in a yearbook.

Swimming in an indoor pool.

Coffee with whipped cream at Hotel Yugoslavia.

Etc.

. . .

Chronology:

On the third of December, 1973, mid-afternoon—though the reader might have been tricked, upon looking through the window, into thinking it was already evening; that was how early it got dark—it is hard to be certain, but probably between 3:00 and 4:00 P.M., The Man Who Shot Liberty Valance appeared in front of our home. At that point we, our family, were disturbed by problems caused by the implacable aging of the human organism. Father was visibly changing. And Mother, though the changes had happened to her much earlier, when rheumatism assailed her joints, was, too. Father grew different. Quieter. More introverted. More pensive. For hours we'd be unable to reach him, to get through. He'd sit staring at the television screen, lounging indifferently in his chair, his right arm flung over the arm of the chair. He wore a gray sweater buttoned up to the throat and a white shirt. The screen flickered, changed color; weak electrical current made the subtitles lose their sharpness, the faces of the actors distort or collapse in two-dimensional space. What was Father afraid of? Or had memories, by some secret route, penetrated his awareness? Mother occasionally averted her eyes and, thinking I wasn't watching, shook her head. Their hands, relaxed on the table, were almost touching. The way they walked was growing similar. Their pain was, too.

From December 3, 1973, to December 16, 1973, therefore, a full thirteen days, The Man Who Shot Liberty Valance stood outside our door. I say days, because we aren't certain where The Man Who Shot Liberty Valance spent his nights. Father expressly forbade us to open the door after 8:30 P.M., after the evening news finished. "People accustomed to everyday danger," he said, "people who live dangerously live differently; they are used to a logic we know nothing of. Noises are, for such people," my father continued, "the speech, the words, the articulation of the universe. They feel danger on their skin, in the air; they sense the smell of danger, its foreboding, and such a man, if he hears a door creak in the night, what will he do? BAM BAM BAM!!!" "But," Mother objected, "he will know that this is our door, that the people opening it mean him no harm . . . " "Will he know?" Father asked.

On December 17, 1973, at precisely 1:15 A.M., a revolver shot reverberated in the hallway of our building. We sat bolt upright in bed. Then we heard noise: the other residents, wakened, had gone out into the hall and were trying to find out what had happened. We joined them. The first thing we noticed was the absence of The Man Who Shot Liberty Valance. His black valise was still there, right by our front door. "He's not here," says Mother. "Who?" asks Father. "The Man Who Shot Liberty Valance is gone!" "He did nothing but bring us trouble," clamored several residents. One woman announced that from the moment that man had appeared at our front door, she constantly feared for her daughter. "How darkly that man would look," she said. Several men went down into the cellar, peered into the bomb shelter, but no, The Man Who Shot Liberty Valance was not there. We climbed up onto the roof. Nothing. In the distance gleamed the lights of the capital city, though they had nothing to do with The Man Who Shot Liberty Valance. Now we were all standing in front of the valise in silence. "Should we open it?" said a retired lieutenant from the third floor. We looked at the lawyer from the first floor. "Sure," he said. Mother leaned over and reached out. At that moment, or rather, at the moment when Mother touched the shiny buckle on the top of the black traveler's valise with the tips of her fingers, the valise turned to dust . . . How? Why? But? Why? Oh! Oh! Oh! We were all surprised. "Now what's this?" said the lawyer. "Look!" someone shouted. We looked down: the dust that at first had made quite a heap had swiftly vanished; it looked as if it were melting, burning of its own accord, without a flame. Oh! Oh! Oh! Oh! Someone reached toward it, but too late: the dust had disappeared, without leaving the slightest trace. "Let's go to bed," said the retired lieutenant after a longish pause. One woman crossed herself surreptitiously. One boy suddenly ran over and spat. One girl said: "I really liked that Liberty Valance." The boy who spat scowled at her with scorn: "He *shot* Liberty Valance, nitwit!" "Oh," the little girl was crushed, "Oho!" She crossed her arms on her chest, and then, so tiny, in a big bathrobe with a hem dragging along the concrete, she reminded us of an angel. Us: Father, Mother, and me.

. . .

Spinoza's thoughts again: "He who would distinguish the true from the false must have an adequate idea of what is true and what is false."

. . .

"I wonder," said Mother, "whether The Man Who Shot Liberty Valance shot himself? That gunshot is what's worrying me. I have been trying to find parallels to the valise that disintegrated. When we touched it, all that was left of it was dust. When he touched it, it was an ordinary traveler's valise, black, made of quality leather. Perhaps someone had touched him in passing? Perhaps that woman who had feared for the fate of her daughter? Maybe the daughter herself, in self-defense? But what about the gunshot? A bullet? An explosion? The terrible propulsive force of gunpowder? A bullet that hurtles with mind-boggling speed from the barrel of a gun? Then where is the shell? If the shell doesn't exist, does The Man Who Shot Liberty Valance exist? Or maybe the revolver went off by itself at a moment of carelessness, at a moment when The Man Who Shot Liberty Valance leaned forward to see something a little more clearly in the dark? Perhaps this was mutual destruction. Eradication. The end. Tata," she addressed Father, but Father didn't hear her. A little later she stopped, seeing that all attempts would be useless, that all paths of communication had long since been cut off, possessed, blocked. She started to doubt whether she had ever said anything, to ask herself how she had managed to spend all those years with him, how she had never understood earlier, why she had permitted all those humiliations, all that degradation and eradication of her being, her speech, her memories. She gave in to the memories, to the years when she was a really little girl, even smaller, even smaller, even smaller, and there she is, trotting about on some flowery meadow, completely unaware that around her is a flowery meadow, flowers, bees, clouds, swallows, snails, shells on the shore, and fish in the river.

. . .

But time is merciless.

. . .

After five brief sounds of the electronic measuring device, the chronometer at the television studio shows that it is precisely eight o'clock.

. . .

The television news.

. . .

Good evening.

. . .

And so forth.

Antonio das Mortes

Antonio das Mortes is standing on the other side of the street, waving at us. A broad, open grin wreathes his face. Father halts, distrustful. "What's this?" he says. "What are all these mythical creatures doing in our lives? First The Man Who Shot Liberty Valance, and now this." He turns to me. "Who is that man?" he asks. "That," I reply, "is Antonio das Mortes." "So, I should wave at him?" inquires Father. "Well," I answer. Father slowly, almost imperceptibly, moves his hand, slowly raises it into the air, pale, translucent, stiff. On the other side of the street, Antonio das Mortes waves all the more frenetically, all the more joyously. His throaty laugh reaches clear across to us. So, we wave at each other for several minutes, and then Antonio das Mortes turns and goes into the City Sweet Shop. Above his dark-as-night black hat swings the barrel of a rifle. Something bulges under the black coat: say, a machete. And that is all we see.

It's true that we keep waving a few more moments, we hear the slam of the door, we feel the gentle shiver of the glass store window. But then traffic, people, sunlight, big clouds in the sky mar our perfect picture. From the depth of the city, columns of workers set out for home. No one pays attention to me. To my father.

. . .

"What's this?" asks my father. "What are all these mythical creatures doing in our lives? Are we not free to act by our own choice? Or is this a question of death at someone else's hands? Why the suffering, why the pain, the defeat, the hope? I read somewhere that even coincidence isn't random, that things happen according to strictly defined laws, rules. What, I ask, what does science want with human lives? All those mythical creatures that appear abruptly disappear just as soon. Are they not the symbol of our resistance? The last attempt at liberation? But who needs the yoke of immortality, who needs eternal repetition of a dream? Oh, Antonio, Antonio das Mortes! Understand this as a request, a proof of human understanding. While you stand on the other side of the street, I offer my hand, I wave at you. Take it, it's yours! But do not forget, Antonio das Mortes: never hesitate! If you think of using your shiny rifle, use it! Shoot! Fire! Only tell me, what is it that is bulging underneath your black coat?

"A machete?"

. . .

The hand lifts high in a slow, soothing movement. It is pale, preserved, translucent. When it reaches the point at which its movement halts, it stops. And at that height it is pale, translucent, decorated with a multitude of bluish veins. Now it starts to move again, to wave (but not with ordinary motions) through the air: left-right, forward-back. No. If you were only a little farther away it would seem that it was still at rest. But this way, so close, you notice that the hand is, nonetheless, moving, moving, but in place. That it's fluttering. That it's trembling. That only the tissue—that's it! that's the word! the nuance!—that the tissue itself is reacting to a stimulus from without. That it's vibrating. It confirms. Hints.

The stimulus is Antonio das Mortes.

The hand raised high is the white flag of surrender.

Surrender is my father.

. . .

The street on which all this happens is not a figment of the author's imagination. Quite the contrary. It is real, cold, tangible. It exists outside the framework of the story, of course—inasmuch as anything exists outside the framework of the story. The careful eye of the newcomer will certainly not miss its almost completely preserved architectural detail, the opulence of the facades almost foreign to this part of the world. Just as he will not miss, we believe, the strange scene which unfolds on that street: one man all in black and, on the other sidewalk, a gray-haired man followed by a boy exchange greetings, wave frenetically as if they are parting forever, as if they will never see each other again. Then the man in black stops waving. He turns and goes into a door over which one can read the words CITY SWEET SHOP, while the gray-haired man and the boy keep waving another few minutes, then stop. Then, suddenly, the street is full of pedestrians, vehicles of the City Transportation Co., jarring sounds, sunlight, distant clouds, and all that, naturally, mars what had until then been a perfect picture. The newcomer quickly looks off and proceeds along his way. While doing so he thinks, if he thinks, that he will not allow himself, in his work-stroll-athletic exercise-relaxation, he will not let such scenes from the lives of other people disturb him. Then—now we are absolutely certain that he is thinking—the fact strikes him that something was bulging under that coat, the coat of the man in black. Naturally, since he is not privy to our story, the newcomer does not suspect a machete. Or rather, he does not suspect anything specific; a little later the event completely disappears from his memory, and he will never, until the day he dies, remember it again.

. . .

The story in which all this happens is a figment of the author's imagination. At this moment, it can take us in dozens of different directions. Will we be able to keep it in check?

Which direction does it mean to take?

. . .

Father halts, leans over to wipe the dust from his shoes. When he straightens up, he notices an unknown man who is waving at us from the other side of the street. "Who is that man?" he asks. "That," I say, "is Antonio das Mortes." Father comes closer, whispers confidentially in my ear: "Do you think it was good that we waved at him?" "Gee," I answer. "He is a criminal, is he not?" "Depends," I say. Father lifts his pale hand high, very high.

. . .

The story in which all this happens is not a figment of the author's imagination. It is genuine, concrete, fragile. It is developing according to its own internal laws, in keeping with its own doubts. One might say that doubt—in its basic mode of existence—is both the cause and the effect. Before you is simply an attempt at presenting this story, in which, as in the painting of any character, mistakes do crop up. The story, the way it is, is only an illusion. Its substance is not known to the author.

. . .

It occurs to the newcomer, while he stands before the shop window of a photography store, that under his wide coat the man in black had a bulge. Staring at high school graduation pictures, the newcomer tries at the same time to think about several other things, which he does not manage to do. So he decides he'd rather look at the photographs, and the man in black and his bulge vanish from his memory. The newcomer is drawn by the face of a girl. Why would a machete interfere with his attention? The newcomer says nothing.

. . .

Until then empty, the street is suddenly filled with pedestrians, cars, newspaper vendors, buses of the City Transportation Co., trash fluttering in the wind (so, the wind is blowing), the neon light of shop windows, sunlight from the sky, distant clouds, and sounds: noise, sirens, the rustling of paper, the rattle of glass, shouts, the screech of automobile tires, laughter.

. . .

Antonio das Mortes is standing on the sidewalk in front of the City Sweet Shop. He turns to the left and to the right, but the street is empty, deserted. Why is the street empty, deserted? wonders Antonio das Mortes. Then, at the end of the street, toward the left, he notices two black dots. Antonio das Mortes raises a fist over his eyes. Exactly, he thinks, the two black dots are people. Before the two black dots see him, Antonio das Mortes starts to wave.

When he stops waving, Antonio das Mortes will enter the doorway over which it says CITY SWEET SHOP.

. . .

"Where do all these mythical creatures in our lives come from?" asks my father. "First The Man Who Shot Liberty Valance, and now this . . . "

"That is Antonio das Mortes," I say.
"Oh!"

. . .

Antonio das Mortes, alone, on an empty street, looks up and watches the sky. High above, it seems to him, he notices a flock of geese in arrowlike flight, but his observations are beyond my powers, out of our reach. Therefore, observations about the flock of wild geese are unknown to the author; they are unknown in the story, just as they are unknown to the flock of geese, high up in the sky.

Then, in the distance, at the bottom of the street, at the foot of the diminutive high-rises, two black dots appear.

The two black dots are people.

. . .

The newcomer turns. What could that be? he wonders, recalling the bulge in the coat of the man in black. Then his attention is attracted by a photograph of a girl with long, blond hair. In his mind's eye, the bulge soon resembles the other folds in the coat; it loses its contours (as does the entire coat) as it enters the nondimensional space of the conscious-subconscious-recall-memory, and quickly shrinks (now we speak of the entire appearance of the man in black) until it becomes a tiny dot, forever lost among the blond hairs of the unknown, long-haired girl.

. . .

There is no one on the empty street. Then, *hop!* Antonio das Mortes; *hop!* here are two black dots, which are people; *hop!* here are endless rows of workers setting out for home; *hop!* here is a bus of the City Transportation Co., the bustle of traffic, and the noise of crowds; *hop!* here are the shouts of the newspaper vendors, neon lights, and distant clouds; and *hop!* now nothing is left. Not even the street.

. . .

"Antonio," says my father. "Oh, Antonio das Mortes, tell me, I implore you, what do you bring *us?* What is it that you're hiding under your broad coat? Is it a decision? Is it death? Death for us? Oh, Antonio . . . Why your silence, why say nothing? Do you think, Antonio, that this is a secret you can surprise us with? Do you think we haven't already experienced dying, that we haven't already learned of death? You are wrong, Antonio, I can tell you that right now. You are wrong if you think so . . . Isn't dying, isn't death . . . ? But you know all that already, why should I repeat it? Tell us your secret, Antonio! Open your beautiful coat! Show us the scythe you wear near your skeleton-body! Wave it! Slice us! Ah, Antonio . . . Ha-ha-ha, Antonio . . . Your arrival could not come at a worse moment, your hopes may be wasted! Who is this Death, what is Death to *us?* Look at our faces, our hands, our limbs! Do they tremble, do they shake, do they change color? No! No! Not a trace of excitement, fear, or anxiety, not a trace of awe . . . We are calm, Antonio, we have never been calmer, while we stand here—here, in the empty street—and wave with wide sweeps through the ruddy evening light. Meeting or parting, do you understand? It doesn't matter?

"Antonio?"

. . .

The story in which all this happens is the product of the story itself. Its characters, its events, its spatial and temporal determinants. Nothing outside it exists. Nothing within it exists. All we have is the story, and the story is unpredictable. It crops up first here, then there. It eludes us, then embraces us. It offers itself up to us, then turns us down.

. . .

The hand raises high in a frenetic movement, so suddenly that, at the moment when the movement ends, the delayed impulses of the nerve threads inform our imperfect senses that the movement continues, that the hand, borne by the force of acceleration, with the formula $a = f/m$, continues to rise, moves, rushes skyward, toward space, the universe, and we, quickly (too quickly, as you shall soon see), raise our eyes along that same path, where, finding nothing, we realize we have been betrayed by our own bodies.

When we seek it out again with our eyes, it is waving already, waving off.

We close our eyes with shame.

. . .

Antonio das Mortes turns, speeds his step, and enters the shop where something is written above the door. The letters, however, are not legible enough; they have faded, eroded by time, peeling under gusts of wind, sun, and rain. Perhaps CITY SWEET SHOP?

How can we be sure?

. . .

The question dies on the lips of the newcomer. The face of the unknown girl steals his attention. What was it that he was thinking a moment ago? Something about a bulge under the broad coat of a man in black . . .

What man in black?

. . .

Antonio das Mortes studies his reflection in the store window. He sees his slender waist, the gorgeous black hat, and *what is that?* a bulge in his coat? Antonio das Mortes turns and thinks . . .

We, of course, have no clue what he is thinking.

. . .

"So that is Antonio das Mortes," says Father. His voice sounds friendly.

. . .

The street on which all of this happens, the city, the intersection, the county boundaries, the boroughs, where does it come from? what procedure was used? what solution? Do boundaries have any specific reality? Why that street, that city, that intersection, etc.? And when it all *hop!* vanishes, what takes its place? Does any event ever cease happening?

. . .

The newcomer halts at the entrance to the park, but without any sort of intent. He had been thinking of something for a while, but of what? Everything in him is overshadowed by the girl's face with the long, blond hair, and he hesitates, he is indecisive. He turns, he looks at the park. To his right: a billboard with two posters, apparently, movie posters. At this distance, we aren't sure what is written on them. The newcomer, without even looking at the billboard, enters the park.

. . .

The lulling street hubbub suddenly stops. In total silence—if such a thing is possible—endless rows of workers disappear before our surprised eyes; so do buses of the City Transportation Co., newspaper vendors, sunlight, clouds, scraps of newspaper, and other things. At that moment we seem to see two black dots in the distance, but no, we are wrong, this is an illusion, our eyes are strained. The street is empty. No one is there.

. . .

"Antonio!" shouts my father, "Antonio!"

His voice fades in the wilderness.

. . .

The story in which all this is happening ceases to exist.

Godzilla the Sea Monster

Godzilla the Sea Monster sits in the shallows of the river. Huge, indescribable tears flow from her eyes. The dumbstruck onlookers come to life only when the salty droplets plunk with a splash into the water. Waiters run around the spacious garden of the Venice Restaurant. The day is lovely, light, the sky a vivid blue, no wind, no clouds. Godzilla the Sea Monster says nothing. That is, for the most part, the entire substance of this story.

. . .

Godzilla the Sea Monster meets my father on the main street, looks at him from above, and says: "How small a man you are!"

. . .

In the story about Godzilla the Sea Monster, we intended to speak about a powerful clash of elemental human passions. Godzilla the Sea Monster was to play the specific symbolic role of all that is negative and destructive in the world around us, such as storms, floods, locusts, very hot weather, ice. My father was to be a vehicle of humanistic tendencies, a supporter of history as theophany, as an enthusiastic viewer of movies on television. Having acquired such features, the main characters were to represent the opposing forces of this world. Godzilla the Sea Monster was to be the vehicle of yin, the female principle of the universe, and my father—graying, wearing eyeglasses, wise—the vehicle of yang, the male principle, the source of light and warmth, of regular monthly earnings, etc., etc. And furthermore, this would illuminate the influences that the philosophy of the Far East exerts on us. We could discourse broadly on the I-ching, *Hagakure,* Lao tse, Zen, and other topics. But even before our first words were out, Godzilla the Sea Monster burst into tears. The scene was irretrievably damaged, feet and feet of movie film were tossed out. Women's tears again seriously undermine the *axis mundi,* the wheel of fortune, the navel of the world.

. . .

Godzilla the Sea Monster watches out of the corner of her eye. My father paces: first in front of her and then behind her. Godzilla the Sea Monster does not turn her head. My father stops. "Why don't you turn?" he asks.

Godzilla the Sea Monster turns. "Pardon?" she says.

. . .

My father and Godzilla the Sea Monster could carry on this sort of conversation:

"Why do you always roam?" my father says.

"Why do I roam?"

"Yes."

Godzilla the Sea Monster hesitates, falters. "I don't know," she says.

"Don't you want peace," asks my father, "security, order?"

"Of course I do," says Godzilla the Sea Monster, *"of course I do!"*

"So?"

"Loneliness . . . "

Father doesn't understand, he raises his eyebrows, then he frowns.

"I am alone . . . "

"Perhaps a minor gynecological procedure?"

"If only someone loved me," howls Godzilla the Sea Monster, and great tears well in her eyes.

But that would take us back to the beginning of the story.

. . .

"Tell me about yourself," Godzilla the Sea Monster addresses my father. "Tell me about your aspirations, your dreams, your family. Surely you have a family? A wife, children . . . You have children? I want to know everything about you, every detail of your life, all the minutiae. Tell me how you spend your days, what you do in your free time, do you play an instrument, what movies you like to watch . . . Then about childhood: where you spent your childhood, how many children there were in the family, how you liked the first day of school, explain to me the games you played, everything. Then the war! What do you think of war? What do you blame war for? What do you like about war? How much have your youthful dreams come true, found fulfillment, played out in the real world? Did you dream, later, as a grown man? Were you capable of adjusting your dreams to reality, so you'd never be disappointed, so you lied to yourself? It all fascinates me . . . Then: your travels. The countries you've visited. The cities you liked best. And why. The ways of thinking you find similar to yourself. And why. The transportation facilities you have used. And why. What else? . . . Have you ever been taken prisoner? How did you get away? How did you get there? Everything, everything! I find everything fascinating! Your first boyhood memories. First love. The first woman you slept with. (Don't try to wriggle out of that one!) The first poet. The first novelist. Tell me about your thoughts on art, the movies you've—no, I asked that already . . . not the movies—tell me about the sculptors you love, the painters, composers, opera . . . Opera! Do you like opera? *Madame Butterfly?* Oh, my darling, my darling! Tell me about your disappointments, your joys, your successes and failures. In a word: tell me about life, about death—no, not about death, not that!—about life, about every day of your life!"

"What is there to tell?" answers my father.

. . .

"Has anyone seen Godzilla the Sea Monster?" asks Father.

"No," says Mother, "I haven't."

"No," I say, "me either."

"What should I do?" asks Father again.

We say nothing. What should we say? We are not the heroes of this story.

. . .

Godzilla the Sea Monster furiously pounds her tail around her. The buildings of Zemun collapse like houses of cards; all that is left of the Tower is a heap of stones. Great waves crash against the river shore; boats crammed with escaping refugees topple like walnut shells; children cry for help. Mothers, where are the mothers? Where are the fathers? Godzilla's toenail knocks over modern high-rises on Karageorge Square. The main street is full of running sewage. The stench of feces rises in the air; dogs sniff corpses frantically; cats make nests in the hair of their dead owners; packs of rats march in orderly columns . . . Is this the end of the world, is that what it is? From smashed tankers some sort of petroleum derivative oozes. Fish float up to the surface belly first. Waterbirds shriek, their wings caked with oil. What was it that irked Godzilla the Sea Monster? Why this unexpected twist to our story?

. . .

"Man is saddled with symbols," says my father. "Psychology, psychoanalysis, semiology, I don't know what else, all of it threatens man's ability to speak. For the question is whether, when he first spoke, man intended a symbol or a precise determinant. The answer to that question will free us of the plague of symbols. Or will it, rather, subject us to them completely? Though it seems to me that we would breathe without them far more easily."

"I, too, am a symbol," sobs Godzilla the Sea Monster. "What will become of me?"

"That doesn't matter," my father soothes her. "It applies only to this story."

. . .

"There is nothing more here for me," says Godzilla the Sea Monster, and as she speaks she hides her eyes, turns her head. "This beautiful city, all these wonderful people, I am not for them, they don't need me, what good can I do them?"

"Don't say that," says my father. "Why the anger?"

"I'm not angry," says Godzilla the Sea Monster, "but, well, I guess, something deep inside me . . . "

Silence.

"Do you think I'm a little overly romantic?"

"Oh, no," says my father, "no. Perhaps you aren't adapted to these times, completely adapted, I mean, like other people. You should be a little firmer, stronger, less sensitive."

"But," says Godzilla the Sea Monster, "you know how much each thing in nature excites me: flowers, birds, the tiniest blade of grass. How can I tolerate it, how can I get ahold of myself? I have more in myself of the romantic than of the neoclassical features, wouldn't you say?"

"Can't you see that your life will last much longer than you expect?"

"I know."

"You'll experience postindustrial society, if I can express myself in those terms."

"I know."

"What do you think: how will it be for you then?"

"Terrible," says Godzilla the Sea Monster. "Terrible."

"And what do you suppose you'll do?"

Godzilla the Sea Monster is quiet for a moment. She thinks,

and then says: "In that case, I'd be better off dying right now!"

"Why?" says my father. "How?"

. . .

We aren't certain, but soon our experience convinces us: yin and yang switch their vehicles. My father sobs while Godzilla the Sea Monster tenderly squeezes his shoulder.

. . .

"I think," says my father severely, "that you shouldn't forget yourself . . . You should show some respect for my age."

"I am older than you," says Godzilla the Sea Monster. "You should respect *me!*"

"My experience is richer, that is what you should value."

"Exactly," says Godzilla the Sea Monster. "What do I know? I don't know anything."

"You've managed to learn something."

"Something? Hatred, nastiness, malice, scorn, envy—there, that's what I've learned! If only I'd been born a thousand years earlier."

"Do you think it would have been better then?"

"Why, of course," says Godzilla the Sea Monster. "First of all: the troubadours. And I would wear an embroidered veil over my face."

"Do you want me to buy you a veil like that?" asks my father.

Godzilla the Sea Monster does not answer right away, she looks at him long and lovingly. "You are the only man I could love," she says. "Did you know that?"

Father turns away; it is obvious how embarrassed he is.

"Don't be embarrassed," says Godzilla the Sea Monster. She lifts her paw and gently turns Father's head toward her.

My father squints.

"If you were only a little younger," says Godzilla the Sea Monster, "if you were only slightly younger . . . "

. . .

Obviously the story about Godzilla the Sea Monster is taking an undesirable turn for us. If we continue in this vein, we run the risk of finding ourselves espousing retrograde ideas. Or, at least as we have done until now, we will not succeed in saying anything in support of positive principles of the ideology of human consciousness. Our effort to express the superiority of the male over the female principle is evident. But then why is Godzilla the Sea Monster becoming stronger and stronger in our eyes while my father is implacably shrinking? Where did we go wrong? Doubting or not believing in the harmony of the universe, in the music of the spheres?

. . .

My father and Godzilla the Sea Monster are standing on the road to Novi Sad. "I am sorry that you are leaving," says my father. Godzilla the Sea Monster turns her head, and touches his forehead with her paw. "You know that I have to go," she says. "I know, but there is always a ray of hope in a person, some crazy belief that no one can take what he loves from him." "You'll make me cry," says Godzilla the Sea Monster. "I love you," says my father. "Must you leave?" "Yes," answers Godzilla the Sea Monster, "the meaning of my existence is in leaving, in abandoning. Do you see what I have left behind me?" Father turns around. Behind them: Zemun, a demolished city, pillars of smoke waft into the air, the distant sobbing of survivors can be heard, the sound of the river flowing back into the riverbed. "New lands await me," says Godzilla the Sea Monster. "A new attempt at softening my nature, at becoming useful and not the destructive force of this universe." "And always behind you leave a man with a broken heart?" "Yes." "But I don't know why I can't stop loving you." "It would have been better if we'd never met," says Godzilla the Sea Monster. "Don't say that," says Father. "At least we spent a few happy moments together."

Godzilla the Sea Monster nods her head. "Yes," she says. "Well then," says Father, "farewell." "Farewell." Father walks away a few steps, then turns. Godzilla the Sea Monster is standing in the same spot. "Go," says my father. "Why aren't you leaving now? Go!" "You go," says Godzilla the Sea Monster. "I will stand here a while longer." "Farewell," says my father. "Farewell." Father takes a few more steps, then turns again. "If you could just send me a few lines now and then?" "Just go," says Godzilla the Sea Monster, "go and don't look back any more!" Father obeys the command and leaves, walking faster and more energetically, and then, from the distance, when he'd almost reached the first demolished Zemun buildings, he hears a voice resembling thunder: "I love you, too, I love you, too, I love you . . . " Father freezes midstep, staring at the ruins. "Why?" he shouts. "Why didn't you say so before? Why the suffering? The pain? Tell me! Why? Why?" "I don't know," he hears the answer, "I don't know!" "I'll turn around," shouts my father, "I'll turn around this minute!" "No," a howl is heard, "no, no don't turn around, no! In the name of our love! No, no, no! Nooooo!" Father does, however, turn around. Before his eyes, in the mist of his tears, his unfulfilled love—Godzilla the Sea Monster—is turning first into Eurydice. Then to stone. Then to Eurydice. Then to stone. Then to Eurydice. Then to stone. Then to Eurydice. And so forth.

. . .

Just as the dots suggest in the yin-yang symbol, nothing is absolute, nothing is pure enough. As much as Godzilla the Sea Monster overlaps with my father, my father overlaps with her. Only together are they an indestructible force of order, change, law, and chance. Separated, they are lost in the distance: the ground disappears beneath their feet, the skies are too far off, emptiness wraps them like a membrane, enveloping them with visible tenderness—though there is no one in the vicinity to see it.

. . .

"So here," says Father, "is my last question." Then he turns to the readers, audience, listeners. "Tell me, if you can, if anyone knows: If life is a battle, if life is movement toward a goal, toward some unknown purpose, what is there to struggle against—meaning or meaninglessness?"

. . .

Silence.

. . .

Against what?

. . .

The silhouette of Godzilla the Sea Monster's body on the horizon. The red color of the setting sun.

. . .

It gets dark.

. . .

Is this the end?

■ □ ■ □ ■

AN ATTEMPT AT DESCRIBING THE DEATH OF RUBEN RUBENOVIĆ, FORMER TEXTILES SALESMAN

THE LINES THAT FOLLOW, PAGES I CANNOT YET PREDICT, events, sounds, things that happen, a place: all of this is just an attempt. The words I'll use, the sentences I'll string together, the questions, the statements: all of it is unreliable, nothing is leading to some known goal, none of it possesses the firmness of the undeniable. What I'll describe is unknown to you; you will never learn what it is I meant to say. The story you will read is yours alone. Between your reading and my intention lie endless rifts of incomprehension and human isolation. The only certainty, the thread which we—with the tenacity of the drowning—will grab for, you and I, is punctuation: the meaning of the comma, the necessity of the period. I could have taken those from you as well, but whom would I have to speak to, then? I am powerless, for words are powerless. You do not understand me, because you understand far too precisely. You and I carry on a dialogue that says nothing to you or to me. You are aware (only) of my pauses, the moments when I breathe air or halt to collect my thoughts; you are aware, therefore, of my humble physiological existence. My mind eludes your grasp, so does my imagination. Words, once they are spoken, die. So you and I share the same fate: like vultures we dig through a graveyard of paper.

Of course, now, once the story has begun, there can be no turning back. Together we will move through its (as yet unexplored, as yet nonexistent) realms, aware, at the same time, that each of us is taking a different path, or, that we use the possibility of metaphor: here we are in a tunnel where we cannot see or hear each other, where we sense one another perhaps, but where fear is so great that we remain forever mute. At the end of the story, at the end of the tunnel in the metaphor, when the light, at first through mist and then with growing clarity, begins to expose us to each other, we will learn how different we are, how inaccurate our guesses had been, and how deceptive our hopes. The metaphor, however, has an advantage over the story: if you're disappointed, you can take the same route back the way you came—to the beginning of the tunnel; a story, once it has been read, no longer repeats: you can't read it backward. You can therefore understand my hesitation to start with the story, to say, for example: Ruben Rubenović, former textiles salesman, is lying in bed and dying; to describe his face: pale, serene, shining, facing the left side of the bed where my father and my mother are sitting, overgrown with a bushy, disorderly beard; to enumerate the striking features of the room: overflowing with things, a large cardboard suitcase on top of the black cupboard, several fat, well-leafed books on the bedside table, a hat on the windowsill, grimy curtains, a garish pitcher covered with a clean white napkin, a wall clock, a color photograph of Jerusalem on the opposite wall; to put forth the uttered words: to say that Mother cries from time to time, that Father (mostly) pats Ruben Rubenović's limp hand, that he himself is experiencing his own death with far more serenity, that I am the silent narrator, that, apart from us, there is no one in the room, and that, at this moment, Father is trying to convince the ailing (dying?) man to eat a section of an orange.

"I can't," says Ruben Rubenović. "Thanks."

"They are juicy," says my father. "Why don't you try?" He fumbles among the pieces of peel. "Here, look," he says, "they're from Israel."

"Shall I make you some tea?" asks Mother.

"No," says Ruben Rubenović, "no need. Thanks."

"Perhaps a little tea might do you good?"

Ruben Rubenović does not answer. He shuts his eyes.

"Ruben," says Mother, nearly standing up.

Ruben Rubenović doesn't open his eyes, but he does ask: "Is it snowing outside?"

Mother continues her initial movement. She stands up and walks over to the window. "Yes," she says, "it is snowing."

Now all of them are separated. It is time, therefore, to use the newly emerging situation—which is still unpredictable—because at the moment when Mother, uttering that last sentence, moves again, the light illuminates her face and slides along the fabric of her dark blue suit (appropriate attire). Her age might not be so obvious to the uninformed reader, who might well wonder, fifty? fifty-two?—which Mother would greet with a smile, for, in fact, she is nearly sixty-three, and her time spent in this room with a man who is obviously dying (is this really her thought?) inflicts inexpressible pain. She can recall, after all, that she has already—and not only once!—had close encounters with what is called death, even her own death, and that she was incomparably calmer. Then what is it that drives her to feel such pity for this small, pale, nearly vanished man? For which man? My father, who sits on a wooden chair right by the bed, is also small, pale, and nearly vanished (whose observation is this?), and his dark suit of heavy English fabric only serves to enhance the impression. Between the man on the bed and the man on the wooden chair there are almost no differences: the same Jewish face, the same curly, gray hair, the same fleshy nose, the same loose lower lip. Who is really dying? Luckily, Mother moves away from the window and a shaft of light touches the frame of Father's eyeglasses, and gleams. Here's a difference; we know who is who again.

When the parquet floor creaks, Ruben Rubenović opens his eyes and follows Mother with his gaze.

"How are you?" asks Father.

"I think I ought to make some tea," says Mother and goes out.

Father waits for the sound of her footsteps to fade, and then, confidentially, he moves his lips to Ruben's face. "Are you afraid?" he asks.

"Ha," says Ruben Rubenović, and for a moment he looks as he used to look in my earlier stories. "Am I afraid?"

"Yes," says Father, "are you afraid?"

"Don't you know what is written in the books? Grieve for those who remain behind . . . "

"That is not what I asked."

"What did you ask?"

Father says nothing.

"Are you afraid?"

"I'd be afraid," says Father.

Ruben Rubenović shakes his head. "You know," he asks, "what a rabbi once said? Repent, he said, the day before you die."

"Yes," says Father.

"How will we know, his pupils asked him, when that day comes?"

"Indeed," says Father, "how would you?"

"Assume," says Ruben Rubenović, "that every day is your last. That is how he answered them."

Father, apparently calm, stands up. But doesn't the very act of standing up suggest a hidden restlessness? Therefore,

I'll exploit the undeniable prerogative of the writer and peek into the most hidden recesses of my father's consciousness, where I'll find, as we expected, chaos, panic, and fear. My father has reached, at the age of seventy, the verge of desperation. To accept the dying (ailing?) man's suggestion that the spirit is the only thing worth paying attention to does not require—or rather, would not require—any particular effort, and I can claim with quite a degree of certainty that in any other situation my father would choose this possibility. *In every other situation*—for he, as a physician, a medical doctor, is mortally (what a paradox!) in love with his body, his secretions and excretions, the working of his glands and limbs, the perfection of the nervous system, the cellular material, subcutaneous tissue, and the cardiac muscle. To claim, of course, that this is the sole reason why he has chosen to live would not do; this same reason informs him of the inevitability of death; it shows him that the heart (to make use, again, of a stylistic figure), like every machine, must one day stop. But to choose the spirit—now my father's thoughts are steadier and easier to follow—means to relinquish the body sooner or later; to choose the spirit at this moment means to relinquish the body at this moment. Death? wonders my father and casts a discreet glance at Ruben Rubenović, former textiles salesman, who, after his last words, has wearily closed his eyes. And at that moment—who knows by what route?—into his consciousness meanders the familiar birthday phrase: *"bis Hundertzvanzig Jahre."* My father is surprised; I am surprised. I can feel how his old sense of confidence begins to return, how the thought of immortality assumes its old contours. Father leans over and with an attentive gesture checks the patient's (dying man's?) pulse, then he touches his forehead. He is sitting up just as Mother, carrying a wide tray, comes into the room. "I made some," she says. Looking at Ruben's rigid face, she stops: "He didn't, did he?" she asks.

"No," says Father. "He's sleeping."

Mother lowers the tray onto the table. "Is he in pain?"

Father looks at her. "Who?" he says.

"What?" Mother asks. "Ruben, of course."

Father takes off his eyeglasses, rubs his eyes, puts his glasses back on, runs his fingers through his hair. "No pain," he says. "He is not in pain."

"What do you mean to say?"

"You grieve for those who remain behind, that is what I mean to say. Grieve for them, and not for the one God has taken to himself; he has gone to a final resting place while we are the ones doubled over by the burden of our sorrow. *It's us.*"

"Is that what Ruben said?"

"Something along those lines," says Father.

"So, why does that infuriate you so much? Because he's right?"

Father does not reply.

"Aren't you pressured by grief, misery, despair, everything?"

"You are just as fearful as I am," says Father.

"Pardon?"

"You are afraid, you're quaking, you're terrified of what will happen in this room!"

"I'm going to wake him up," says Mother. "He shouldn't drink his tea cold."

"Answer me," demands Father.

"Ruben," says Mother. Then louder. "Ruben!"

"Don't wake him," says Father, "before you answer me."

"I don't want to answer you."

"You must!"

Mother carefully closes the teapot, silent.

"Mama," says Father. "Little woman?" And he begins to cry.

My mother's next actions are almost predictable: she pushes the tray away, goes over to where Father is sitting, and draws his head to her breast. Father sobs, he speaks garbled words while Mother gently runs her hand through his gray (we've already said that) hair. My father's actions, however, which follow as soon as I punch the colon key, elude both your and my predictions, and convince us again of how difficult our common efforts are: Father suddenly breaks free of Mother's embrace, you see, and comes across the room and addresses—whom?—me. Although his words are spoken softly and his sentences confused and incomplete, I understand that he is offering me some kind of deal, that (actually) he is insisting that I accept his request, stressing as undeniable the fact that he is my *parent,* and that I am obliged to show him at least a modicum of respect. "Do you see," he says, "what you have done to that woman, what pain you've caused her? She is your mother, after all. And you've hurt me, too. Look, I'm crying. Isn't that enough? Must you continue? This story is, after all, nothing but an experiment, that man (he means Ruben Rubenović, author's note) needn't die; you can interrupt all of this, or continue at some other time when we have all had more rest, when we can take it more easily. It isn't easy," he goes on, "to look death straight in the eyes, to face this single certainty, at least not at my age, perhaps at yours death means something else, perhaps all of this means something else, different than what we see in it, but at my age . . . Listen," he whispers, "toss it all out, you haven't written much, and get us out of here. Furthermore, I don't know any Ruben Rubenovićes, this is pure fiction, a figment of your imagination, some sort of prototype of a Jew, right? So why should we be suffering and agonizing because of some figment, because of *your* imagination, when reality is different, truer, nicer. Let him (Ruben Rubenović, author's note) die, I don't care, but us, let *us* leave. I am your father, and don't you forget it. Do you know how all this will end if you don't do something soon? I demand, I am your *parent,* I demand that you do something this minute, that you desist with this comedy of writing and that you give us back the dignity we used to have!"

"Tata," Mother says suddenly and stops holding him, "Tata!"

Father, jerking awake, gets up without a word.

"Do you hear me?" asks Mother.

"Pardon?" answers Father. "Pardon?"

"It looks," says Mother, "as if Ruben Rubenović has died."

Isn't this proof, yet again, of unpredictability: the climax of the story at a time when the author, the characters, and the reader least expect it? Perhaps it all happened too fast, but who knows the paths and ways of death? That Father professionally establishes death while Mother sits staring (as they say) into her own future, isn't this confirmation of reality? But what is reality? Didn't Father, in the lines above, contradict the reality of this story and call everything a figment of the imagination by saying that reality is different, truer, nicer? You, of course, note that even the veracity of *his* statements is questionable, for nobody could be in two places at once: how could Mother be holding Father and running her fingers through his hair while Father is standing and talking with you (with the author, author's note)? Someone, you say, someone in this story must be lying. But that means that you, too, acknowledge the existence of a story, you blur the question of reality even further, you lead all of us to a greater quandary. The question, therefore, is not what is reality? but rather, is there reality? Who is the writer here, who the reader, who the characters of this story? With what right can any of us claim that the role we have been given is really our role? The reader is an author; the author is the main character; the characters are readers, authors, and innocent bystanders. The story has originated on its own, just as death originates on its own (a successful comparison); death, however, precedes life; the story is preceded by what? This section has too many questions, too few answers; no one is satisfied. Father stands by the window and from time to time turns toward the bed where the motionless body of Ruben Rubenović, former textiles salesman, is lying; Mother is also motionless, though more relaxed than tense, on a wooden chair right next to the bed; the room does not make a sound and is gradually filling with twilight, silence, and chill; a boy, who was not mentioned earlier, left to his own devices in the corner of the room, has almost totally retreated behind the old-fashioned black cupboard, where he will soon be overcome by fear and sleep; the tea, poured into a deep teacup, is cold and covered with a clear scum; a little girl, who, for the same reason (which?), was not mentioned earlier, is crying soundlessly, dressed in a supernaturally white dress (if she weren't human she could play the part of an angel perfectly, though she has no wings and her hair should be longer; as she is, human, she is merely a mute witness of horror that she will—she guesses—witness frequently); the on-duty physician, who comes with the ambulance, signs the death certificate, presses an official stamp, lights up a cigarette; the wall clock ticks. This section is too long, clumsy, overflowing with unexplained details, unconvincing, and unclear. The ends of the story are no longer in the author's hands; warnings to those who are interested appear in their full glory. First the reader has abandoned us, now the father and mother are taking the same route. What's more, Father stands at the door and addresses—whom?—me, stressing that he was right, that my imagination (this time he calls it imagination again) has brought only evil, and that what I have done to him, my parent, then to Mother, then to my sister and myself, is unacceptable. "Not only have you taken away the dignity that belonged to us," he says, "you no longer intend to return it." His eyes are red; he suffers from chronic conjunctivitis; his words contain multiple meanings; finally we know who the boy and girl are—they are me (the author, author's note) and my sister when we were small. There is an error of logic, *irrationality,* committed when introducing these two children to this story. They, as children, were witness to a different death; my sister, furthermore, was not present at the death of Ruben Rubenović, former textiles salesman, nor did she even know that Uncle Ruben (that was what she called him) was dying. Since she vanished as soon as she was mentioned, Father's words eradicate all possibility of believing in the existence of angels, a belief that, given the way events unfolded here, was completely plausible. A confusion of realities, a dilemma about the existence and appearance of reality, will not resolve this. The author of this story picks up the boy (himself when he was a child), and in a few more steps he makes it to the end of the tunnel. He entered the tunnel long ago and is no longer certain whether he is in metaphor, reality, or cleverly composed narrative prose. The view that stretches before his eyes (blinded by the sun) is idyllic, the air fresh, the breeze mild. The boy in his arms also opens his eyes. The author and the boy look at one another for a long time, then the author lets the boy down onto the ground and offers him a hand. The boy first turns back and regards the tunnel, then sees the forest in front of him. The author, with a few select sentences, tries to explain to him that making one's way through metaphors is the only form of reality available to the two of them, their goal in life, so to speak, and that after the tunnel they have to pass (make their way) through a forest, and after the forest, who can tell? The boy says that he doesn't know what a metaphor is, but that he is interested in what lies deep inside the forest, and so the two of them, holding hands, vanish among the trees nearest to us.

▪ ▫ ▪ ▫ ▪

PICTURE, WINDOW

ON SATURDAY NIGHT I DREAMED OF HIM AGAIN. CONTRARY TO reality, he was alive in my dream and I was dead. I lay on the bed, a short white sheet draped over my thighs, my feet and ankles absorbing the remainder of light. My father sat on a peeling kitchen stool and sobbed. Misery marked his face; he brushed his eyebrows or nose now and then, wiping errant tears; now and then he'd rest his hands on his knees, he'd shake his head in stark disbelief. Then he took up a prayer book and began reading. I saw him rock back and forth while the Hebrew words caught in his throat. You could hear his throat was dry. Then he choked, he began coughing, and his glasses tumbled down his chest, over his lap, to his knees, onto the floor.

In the morning I went to the cemetery.

"Why are you doing this to me?" I asked him.

I stood in front of the broad tombstone still covered in dewdrops. "Why are you doing this to me?" I repeated.

He said nothing.

"If you're nursing a grudge," I said, "tell me."

Behind me something rustled.

I turned, but there was no one there. I went over to a walnut tree and peered among its branches the way I peek under women's skirts. I thought of squirrels. I'd like to see squirrels carrying walnuts to their lairs, if there are any walnuts at this time of year and if there are any squirrels.

No sign of life.

So I went back to my father's grave.

On the other side of the path I saw a fresh mound with a wooden marker. On it was written "Flora Montijas, 1903–1985."

When we buried my father here a few years ago, this whole section of the graveyard was uninhabited. But now, if I am not wrong, there are only a dozen plots left. When they are taken, the cemetery will cease to live. Jews will have to go elsewhere to rest in peace, to await the moment when the Messiah returns, when the Golden Gate in the city walls of Jerusalem will swing open all by itself. Under the condition, of course, that the Messiah doesn't miss the moment. Because if he misses it this time, as he may well have done on a number of occasions in the past, nothing will save us.

"Your sense of catastrophe," my father used to say, "is so unnatural, so artificial, that it can only be a caricature of itself, a parody."

"Perhaps," I shrugged, "but I have always been attracted by the differences in things, what makes them distinct."

Father dismissed me with a flick of his hand.

"If you want things to be different," he said, "then first you have to make them the same. Only then can you take up changing them."

By which he meant, first you have to be like everyone else, and only when you're good at that can you begin to be different.

There is a certain order to things that cannot be changed.

I walked a little way off from father's grave and found a pebble of an unusual shape. I placed it on the edge of the grave, stroked the marble with my fingers, then my lips, then I left.

I closed the cemetery gate behind me. A tram rumbled by. First one gypsy woman, then two more, offered me bouquets of flowers. There weren't any more copies of the daily paper at the newsstand. I had a yen for a hot dog. The grocery store was well stocked. Barbers, idle, spun in their own chairs. On the steps lay an empty juice package. The traffic lights adapted to the traffic like chameleons. My eyes stung. I picked at my ears. The postman had no cap. Certain crafts are dying out. There was a smell of dust in the air.

"Pictures make the world," my father said.

At that time he was already ailing, his skin was wan, his eyes had lost their luster, his hair was thinning, his fingers refused to obey him, his belly produced unpleasant sounds, his mouth was twisted, his gums were receding so his false teeth slipped, fell out, escaped down the pillow damp with sweat.

"The window is shut," said the patient in the next bed.

The room they lay in was small, cramped, two beds and a coatrack, bedside tables, a sink, two chairs without armrests, curtains, a photograph of some coastal town on the wall.

My father twisted his head to see the patient in the other bed better.

"What window?" asked my father. "What is he talking about?"

"He thought you meant 'window,' 'picture window,'" I said.

"The guy's a lunatic," my father said, and tried to snatch his teeth.

Lunatic or no, there was truth in what he said. The world may be made of pictures, but the window is shut, or rather, the time has come, the moment is upon us for the window to close and the pictures to end. No more pictures, no more world.

My father went on dying like a shrew. He refused to be covered and pushed away all the blankets. He insisted that he was hot and that he had to lie naked in bed. Into his limp penis they jammed a tube that diverted his urine to a clear plastic bag. Madness gleamed in his eyes, which was actually a lucidity we will never know in our lives. Our visits turned into futile attempts at getting him to eat, to lie in bed peacefully, to take his medicine, and he resisted, howled, flailed, kicked off blankets, tore off his undershirts, turned over plates, dumped out glasses of water.

Two or three years later, when at the table, I recognized him in a gesture of mine, his movement. I tried to repeat it, but I couldn't quite recapture the likeness. Later, at unpredictable moments, it would happen that I'd recognize him in me. While I was dropping off to sleep with my hands crossed under my head I'd feel I was he, and if in the rare darkness of the room I'd open my eyes, I'd see the world the way he saw it. The grimace of the face I'd glimpse in the mirror, in passing through the front hall, was his; it belonged only to him. In those flashes he lived instead of me, coming back the way I will come back in the body of my son.

Every person has a father. Every father had his father. Etc.

"If you want to be sure of yourself," my father said, "first you have to overcome your insecurity. Only when you see what it means to be unsure can you accept certainty."

When I woke up I lay there, eyes closed. I heard every familiar sound in our apartment: the ticking of the wall clock, the splashing of water in the bathroom, the rattle of window glass as a bus passed. I was afraid to open my eyes. What if I was my father waking up? With the fingers of my right hand I touched my left arm, then with the fingers of my left hand I touched my right wrist. This could be me, but then again it might be someone else. I touched my face: forehead, eyelids, cheeks, lips, chin, nose. Is it necessary to open one's eyes to be sure of who you are? I stopped pressing my eyelids shut and through my lashes I saw the morning light. Then I lifted my head and saw, at the foot of the bed, my feet. They clenched, they straightened. I still have a lot to learn, I thought. That is how the day began.

■ □ ■ □ ■

JERUSALEM

I FIRST SAID "JERUSALEM" WHEN I WAS ELEVEN YEARS OLD. We were sitting around the large dining room table and closely following my father's index finger as it traveled over a map of the Balkans. "Belgrade, Niš, Skopje, Gevgelia," said Father, following his finger, and then he lifted it from the map as if the border were real. "Salonika, Athens, Piraeus," he added. "Here," he tapped Piraeus with his fingertip, "we will board a ship, and then"—he flipped several pages until he arrived at a map of the Mediterranean—"Rhodes, Cyprus, Haifa." He looked at us carefully, one by one, Mother, my sister, then me. "And, God willing, we shall see Jerusalem." The last word fell upon me, draped me like a cloak (which I was to recognize, many years later, in the sky above Zion), and I felt called upon to repeat it. I said "Jerusalem." Meanwhile, Father's face twisted, crumpled, and leaning on his hands—which whitened from the weight of his body—he began to cry.

Memories are, of course, tricky, even though they are all we have to feel that we truly exist. Jerusalem, the word, had undoubtedly traversed our apartment before that day. Father certainly must have mentioned it in conversations, in commenting on the daily news or while he was dictating to Mother a letter for our relatives. Perhaps he said it while he was reading a prayer for the holidays, blessing the bread and the wine. I recently leafed through his old prayer books and tried in vain to make out the Hebrew letters that make the word "Yerushalayim." Letters that lay mute like my father, like my ignorance, which has made of me a certain stranger.

I did learn a few things. One of them was that Jerusalem may be the only city to which every visit is like dying. Every time I have left it I feel as if a part of me has died. Sometimes a body part, sometimes an elusive feeling that circles around the heart, sometimes one of the many layers of the soul. I talked about this with Father. He halted in the middle of the room and spread his arms. "Regarding Jerusalem," he said, "I am a living corpse." Even then I was taller than he was, and I mused how I could easily put my arms around his waist or his rear and lift him high into the air. I carried him, but only when he was dying: twice helping ambulance drivers, once up the stairs, a second time down, and then many times all by myself, all those days while he lay helpless in bed. Nothing of his earlier lightness was left then. He had wasted away, indeed, but his body seemed to grow denser—it changed its specific weight, it dragged everything downward with it. I carried him from the armchair in the living room to the bed in the bedroom, and when I set him down my arms would still be under his body. I would lay my head on his chest and listen to its deep silence.

It couldn't go on for long. Judging from the documents, my father died within two or three months. Judging from memory, his death arrived from afar, like a traveler riding on a slow horse, like a huge wave whose tousled crest rears over us like a cobra. I have never seen a cobra. I am relating all of this only because I believe that simple things (death) can be invalidated using complex structures (storytelling), though I should have figured out a long time ago that simplicity is more convoluted than any complexity. There is no labyrinth more twisted than a straight road connecting two small towns along the shore of the same river.

Whatever the case, my father died and I kept on going to Jerusalem. One clear night, for instance, I stood on the flat roof of the Catholic orphanage and looked out into the square courtyard of the adjacent Arab house. The door was open, a curtain of colorful beads was hanging in the doorway, and light in the form of an elongated trapezoid lit the stone doorstep and a pair of worn slippers. Another time, when I was walking up a steep street, I watched the powerful thighs of a woman who was carrying a basket filled with fruit. Everything changed on the downhill slope. The sun was setting and its rays poked in under the eyelids. I remembered how I went to a church with white walls, only above the altar was Jesus' figure, framed by a circle of a darker color. And in the twilight above the noisy street I sat on the terrace of an Arab restaurant and ate hummus and pita bread.

All this turns to crumbs with the ineffable yet familiar taste of death. That night when my father suffered a stroke, I woke up in the moist Tel Aviv night and tried, in the dark, to remember what had jerked me awake. I heard how my father moaned, I rushed to get up, and then the space between our beds seemed to stretch. I felt as if I were slogging endlessly through darkness, but I may have only been bouncing in place. Father's sheet was hovering in the air like a flying carpet, and what had looked from afar like an oar was, in fact, his arm. It hung by the bed, white and unreal, and the tips of his fingers brushed the floor. He must have heard me come over, because he turned his already twisted face toward me and lifted his other arm, grabbed me by my undershirt, yanked me to him, the seams began to rip, you could clearly hear in the darkness how the fabric was tearing. I had to kneel, and his head nestled onto my shoulder. I took his head in my arms and my fingers felt the tiny curls of his hair. I thought how it would be best if we could fly out the open window on that sheet, straight into the night, straight to Jerusalem. I've always wanted to see Jerusalem from great heights.

Then on my stomach and thighs I felt the pressure of his

limp arm, and I realized that death had already moved in on him. Perhaps there, in Tel Aviv, on the shore of the Mediterranean, I should have been thinking of crabs living in snail shells: this would be a fitting image for the life that remained in the unliving shell of his body. Instead of this, in my mind's eye I saw the whiteness of Jerusalem stone, then that unreal moment of early evening when the entire city turns to flaming gold.

It is odd: sometimes when something vanishes it is enough to close my eyes; but sometimes you have to open them. This world is two-faced and imperfect.

There can be no comfort—I am certain—in this. A month later I brought my father back to Belgrade on Swissair. Jews used to come to the Land of Israel to end their lives there; now they go to end them somewhere else. Oh, that is just one more of my fabrications. Actually, the soul of every Jew dies in Jerusalem, regardless of where the body happens to be. My father's body finally gave up the ghost at a Belgrade clinic. It was late summer, the beginning of early autumn, and people were still going around in shirtsleeves. I remember that I suddenly felt weightless, horribly weightless; I even wondered whether I might fly. And then someone phoned and said he had died, and words suddenly became pointless.

PART II

▪ ▫ ▪ ▫ ▪

MY WIFE HAS LIGHT EYES

"THIS WILL BE A SIMPLE STORY," I THINK, "AND IT WILL HAVE no compound sentences."

"Don't be silly," says my wife. "That sentence is already pretty compound."

I turn and look at her. I see her as I've never seen her before, but she doesn't know it. "What are you," I say, "a mind reader?"

My wife doesn't answer. This is one of her talents. Instead she says something else. "If you have lied to the reader in your very first sentence, how can you expect your reader to believe your next one?"

I stare at the blank sheet of paper in front of me. "I didn't lie to my reader," I say, "because I haven't written anything down yet."

"But you thought it," says my wife.

This resembles one of those exhausting marital spats from the stories and novels of John Updike. I have no time for that. So I don't beat around the bush. "According to you," I say to my wife as if she'd written the gospel, "according to you," I repeat for the sake of inner rhythm, "prose is supposed to be truthful."

"Are you asking or declaring?" asks my wife.

"Asking."

"Declaring," she says.

"In that case," I say, "if I were describing you I would

have to write, 'the nipples on her breasts hung unevenly,' or 'the wrinkled skin on her neck,' or 'her scrawny legs laced with veins.'"

"So?" says my wife.

Her poise is legendary. Which goes without saying.

"Wouldn't it bother you," I ask, "if people knew the truth about you?"

"Of course not," says she, "because they never believe that what they're reading is true anyway."

That does it! I stand up to evade pointless description but still I manage to tell her she is overdoing it. "First you tell me I have to be truthful so my readers trust me," I shout, "and then you tell me they don't believe me anyway! Why?! Can you tell me why?"

My wife doesn't blink an eye. Her poise is legendary, etc. She says, "We are speaking of two different kinds of believing. I don't see why you're shouting. It is the writer's job to persuade the reader of the sincerity of your intentions, but still the reader doesn't believe the reality of fiction. Fiction is fiction—and nothing more, right?"

"What have we here?" I say. "Where did you read that? In Eagleton's book on literary theory?"

Now I am really angry, angry and thirsty. I'd go off into the kitchen to get a glass of water, but I'm worried that I'll miss something.

"You won't miss anything," says my wife, and tweaks at the strap that has slipped off her shoulder. The strap that always slips when she means it to, simply a neat way of drawing attention to herself, of channeling it, funnel-like, to the curve of her shoulder.

"To the mole on my shoulder," says my wife, "which has been kissed by many."

"Fine," I say, "to the mole on your shoulder, but how can it be that you know my every thought? Who is protagonist in whose story here? Or are you," I shout, "really a witch?"

"Cut the crap," says my wife.

This is another of her talents: mastering a situation, picking the right word, eliminating l'art-pour-l'art-ism in any way, shape, or form.

"Listen," I say winningly, "it is still not too late. We can work something out, we can figure out where we're each coming from, we can state precisely how it will start and how it will finish . . . "

"If there is something I do not want in life," says my wife, "it is certainty."

"But I am not talking about life," I say.

My wife shakes her head. "If you have literature in mind," says she, "then you are in real trouble. Certainty is death for literature."

I stop moving, or rather, first I start because just a moment ago I said I was standing still, then I stop moving. Is my wife right after all? (She claims she always is, but I refuse to put that in writing.) Perhaps certainty in its literal sense of the word is indeed "death for literature"? I start to move again but cannot figure out whether I am on my way into the kitchen to drink the glass of water mentioned before or am going back to my desk where I was sitting before my wife began to read my thoughts.

"All in all," says my wife, taking up her knitting, "writing is a waste of time. What did you plan to write, anyway?"

"Oh," I say, "something pretty simple."

"Like?"

"Like: once there was a woman, and after four, no six, after six years of marriage, in the autumn, she runs into an old boyfriend, a sentimental, burned-out professor, abandons her husband and child, a boy of five, maybe a little girl, too, and goes off with the professor. The final scene takes place along some dusty road. At one end stands the husband. The wife touches her husband on the cheek. She crouches down in front of the child, the child blinks, and then she walks away, slowly, almost staggering, and then she starts to run to the professor, who is waiting for her with outspread arms. Then the child says: 'Where is that man taking Mommy?' At that moment the first leaf flutters down from a tree."

"Awful," says my wife. "Where did you come up with *that?*"

Which was another one of her talents: asking a question that needs no answer.

"Tsk, tsk," she says and takes up new knitting. No, crocheting. My wife crochets, her fingers following some new pattern. "Tell me," she says, "where do you plan to submit this?"

"Literary Word," I say.

She looks at me, surprised, which is pretty unusual for my wife. Anyway, her hair is brown, her eyes are light, her knees sometimes rub when she walks, from some childhood disease. "They won't accept it," she says, finally.

Now I am really aggravated. "It's not enough that you're a vixen and a witch," I shout, "now you want to be a literary critic, too!"

"And why not?" says she.

I keep shouting, "Are you going to start telling me what sort of story I'm supposed to be writing? Is that what you want?"

She takes up her embroidery, spreads out the cloth. It shows a classic household scene: a woman in a (rather short) fluttering skirt stirs food in a large pot. Smoke is wafting from the pot, a smile is frozen on the woman's face, the index finger of her free hand is raised in warning.

"What is this," I howl, "a message or something?"

"There are no messages," says my wife in a steady voice, "there are only people who believe in messages."

This has never dawned on me. Is there truth in it? I feel myself relaxing. I'd take a seat but I can't remember whether I am standing in the story or not.

"Do you want to hear *my* story?" asks my wife.

"Yes," I say. "I do."

"This one is about a man," she says, "middle-aged, ordinary. One day when he goes out, maybe on his way to work, I don't know how important that is, but this day, when he gets, say, to a crosswalk, he realizes that everything is the way it is. Everything is the way it always has been and the way it always will be. Nothing changes, or rather if something does change it becomes, at the same time, the way it was. Because of this the man doesn't go to work, I mean, he doesn't go where he was headed; he goes home. When he unlocks the door and walks into the room, say, first into the front hall, then into the room, he sees that things are the way they are, that he is wading through an unchanging mire. He sits in an armchair, stares at a spot on the ceiling, and then he hears the doorbell. Someone is ringing the doorbell at his front door. He gets up, walks over to the door, asks who's there. No one answers. The man doesn't hear anything outside. A moment later the bell rings again. He opens the door. The hallway is empty. The man walks over to the bannister around the stairwell and peers down, but then the door to his apartment slams shut, swung by a draft of air. He is left in the hallway, without a key, alone. He walks to the door, listens, lifts his hand, and rings."

"And?"

"And nothing," says my wife. "That is the end of the story."

"And you think they'll like it?"

"Yes, I do."

There is something to that last scene: the man in the hallway ringing with no one in his apartment. To myself I acknowledge the value of the scene, but not aloud.

My wife looks at me. Her eyes are light and large, but when she comes, the lids flutter, her eyes roll back, and I see nothing but the whites, a flash of white between swaying lashes.

"Say something," says my wife.

"If I were that man," I say, "and if the door were closed,

and if you were sitting inside, here, where you're sitting now, and if I were to ring the bell, would you open the door?"

She folds up the cloth with the embroidery. I have seen these movements of hers before—last time when I was writing a story for *Politika,* and before that, too, this spring, for instance, when I confessed a couple of things to her.

I'd repeat the question, but that technique has been so overworked in literature and the movies that I opt for silence.

No amount of silence, however, can shield us from the truth, because we all know, and have long known, her reply.

"No," says my wife, "I would not."

■ □ ■ □ ■

A MOVIE ON TELEVISION

I VISITED MY FRIEND A FEW DAYS AGO. ON WEDNESDAY I phoned him, or was it Thursday, and said we'd come over on Saturday, or Sunday. We: my wife and I.

More than a year had passed since the last time we were together, and now the appearance of his apartment surprised me agreeably. I don't recall how his apartment looked earlier, or even whether I had ever been there, but the look of this place made a nice impression. Everything was in cozy, pastel colors; the curtains reached the floor; the floors were carpeted with soft rugs; the furniture was simple and comfortable; the dishes were heavy, solid, and sat in my hand as if they were made for my hand only.

My friend and I sat next to each other, in armchairs stitched with wide seams. Across from us, on the couch, sat our wives. Two or three times that evening my friend gave my wife measured looks that sent shivers down my spine. I would love to have someone look at me that way. As far as his wife was concerned, I only looked at her once. I didn't find her hips appealing, if those were her hips, though I sensed the line of her thigh was the way I like to see it when I see a thigh, naked, on a sheet, partly covered by a blanket. Beauty is in presentiment, in hints, in expectation of the whole. Not in big hips.

Someone else could have sat between the two of them, that is how large the couch was. They leafed through the most recent issue of *Burda,* or perhaps the fall *Vogue,* and because of the space between them they sat awkwardly angled, twisted. My wife lowered her finger onto a page as if she wanted to show that she had decided on one of the styles. Then my friend's wife pointed to something on the page, though it may not have been the same style.

My friend sighed.

I glanced at him out of the corner of my eye and thought that he was thinking about my wife. I wondered whether he was thinking about her the way I think about her. I always imagine her in specific poses, her head flung back, her head must be flung back when I picture her, but for him, in his thoughts, maybe her head is stiff, or straight, or who knows where.

"More rum?" his wife said.

We were drinking rum and Cokes.

"Why not?" said my friend. He got up and went to a side table where the bottles with drinks stood. While he walked around the room and poured us rum, you could hear quiet clinking, the ring of glass. My friend's hands, it seems, were trembling.

He sat again in his armchair and shot me a polite, hospitable grin.

My wife turned a page.

Many years earlier, my friend and I had been to the coast together. What I mean to say is that we were hardly such strangers that we had to sit there silently one next to the other, swirling the drinks in our glasses with little jerks. We could have talked, but not now, not with our wives sitting across from us. Before we set out that evening, while I was shaving in the bathroom, I had formulated (to myself, of course) sentences I might say to him if we had even a minute to ourselves. But it seemed that we would never end up alone; his wife left a few times, but mine stayed in the room. The *Burda* lay on her lap like a weight.

What I wanted to tell him was pure man talk, memories

that bond men no matter how great the distance. I don't believe that our wives would enjoy hearing this.

I coughed. In the general warmth of my friend's living room even a cough sounded warm.

I said, "Do you mind if I roll a joint?"

My friend and his wife exchanged glances. It seemed to me, though I'm not certain, that she just barely nodded her head.

"Why would we mind?" he said.

They watched closely as I took out the papers and the aluminum foil with the hash from my pocket. The papers were pretty, yellow, with little gold stars scattered on them. I had never managed to figure out the pattern. The pattern may be so complex that the same pattern of stars repeats only on the seventeenth joint, or on the thousand and first.

"I hope I haven't surprised you with this," I said.

"No," said my friend, "why?"

His wife never took her eyes off my hands.

"I didn't know you smoke," said my friend, "that's all."

"I didn't know you don't," I said.

No one laughed.

"I only smoked once," he said. "Nothing happened."

My wife barged in. "That is what they all say at first," she said. "When the two of us first smoked together, I knelt for two hours on the floor and kept saying nothing is happening."

I kept my mouth shut, though I could have said something. I sprinkled tobacco on the paper and unwrapped the aluminum foil. When she and I *first* smoked together, it was not her first time. Nothing kept happening to her with someone else, not with me.

"Lighter," I said finally. I felt like a surgeon.

My friend handed me a lighter. The kind you throw away when it's used up.

"I've never tried," said his wife.

My wife looked her straight in the eyes. "Don't be scared," she said, "nothing will happen."

"I'm not scared," said the wife of my friend.

I warmed up the hashish and began to crumble it. The dark crumbs mingled with the little curls of tobacco.

"If I remember correctly," said my friend, "someone at the time said we were smoking 'Turkish' or something like that."

"This is much better," I answered. "This is from Lebanon."

"May I watch?" asked my friend.

I handed him the knob of hash, and he took it gingerly, as if it were glass, or lead crystal.

"Does it cost a lot?" said his wife.

"Twenty thousand dinars a gram," my wife said. "At least."

I made a filter from an old bus ticket. I picked up the paper and noticed that my hands were trembling, too. I licked the edge of the paper and shaped the joint. I squeezed the tip; I crumpled a couple of the stars and mused that the universe expands and contracts in the same way.

"Hardly cheap," said the wife of my friend, as if she had been thinking all that time about the price of hash.

"Nothing's cheap nowadays," said my wife.

"So true," said my friend. He looked at me. "Do you want a light?" he asked.

I leaned over and he flicked on the lighter. I puffed once or twice, got the joint going, and offered it to him.

He took it like melting ice cream. "What do I do now?" he asked.

I told him: "Inhale the smoke, hold it in for a minute, then breathe it out."

He nodded and breathed in. After a few minutes he looked at me again, but that time I nodded. He let his breath go. "What now?" he said.

"Pass it to me," said my wife.

I watched how the joint suddenly, yet slowly, moved away from me and toward the lips of my wife. I glanced to the right and saw the lips of my friend's wife.

"Are you sure that nothing will happen to me?" she spoke.

"Inhale the smoke," said my wife, "and don't worry."

My wife has a way with people.

I looked at my friend: he was already grinning. Then the grin vanished from his face. When I turned, I saw that his wife was going over to him.

She said, "Maybe I should put some water on for coffee." She left the room before we had a chance to respond.

I licked my finger and moistened the paper, which was burning crooked. The stars had gone out on its sky, pretty soon dark night would fall.

Then my friend smoked again, then my wife came over, knelt, took the joint, and stayed sitting on the floor.

I said, "Does your wife want some more?"

"Where is she?" answered my friend.

"Making coffee," said my wife.

My friend shrugged.

I got up and took the joint into the kitchen. My friend's wife was pouring coffee into heavy, pastel coffee cups. She inhaled again, gave me back the joint, and took the tray with the cups on it into the room.

I was left alone there in the kitchen. There were two ashtrays on the round white table. I tried to remember how my friend's kitchen used to look. I remembered a kitchen, but I wasn't certain whether it was his. I went to another door, not the one back into the living room, and tried to open it. It was locked. I went back to the table and stubbed out the joint in one of the ashtrays.

When I came back into the room, first I heard the television, then I saw it. My friend was still sitting in his place. His wife was crouched in the corner of the couch. My wife was sitting on the floor. "Sit down," she said when she saw me.

I sat down.

My friend slowly turned and stared at me. The whites of

his eyes were bloodshot. He put his hand on mine and squeezed it.

"How are you doing?" I asked his wife.

"I don't feel much of anything," she said.

My wife grinned.

"Next time," I said, "next time it will be better."

Then the movie began. At first it was slow moving, the plot was spread out on several different story lines, and then everything began to speed up. Heroes, as far as I could tell, switched in the middle of the tensest scene. Two women, one old and one young, did not succeed in finding a common language. Horses romped on some mist-filled meadow. Then everything moved from the countryside to the city. Tall, uniform buildings promised nothing. Along the sidewalk the wind blew leaves, old newspapers, a man's hat, which no one tried to catch. Afterward we found ourselves in someone's messy apartment. The table was covered with leftover food. The closet gaped empty. On the umbrella stand in the front hall there was only one ragged umbrella. The rug in the first room was frayed. The other room was lit with meager light. The bathroom, in passing, suggested drastic neglect. The third room was the master bedroom. We saw a wide, old-fashioned bed, then the naked feet of a man and a woman, then their bodies covered only with a sheet of dubitable cleanliness, then his bare, hairy chest and her bare breasts, then, in the end, their faces, grotesquely misshapen. His swollen tongue protruded from his open mouth. The camera moved slowly upward, and we could see a painting of some lake in the Alps, and around it a pine woods, and in the woods, on the minutely drawn meadow, the minuscule figure of a deer. The deer was certainly waiting for its doe. We couldn't see it; I was just guessing. Then the letters said that it was the end.

"Ugh," said my friend's wife, "I could barely stand it."

My wife got up off the floor and began to stretch. She stood on her toes, put her hands high above her head, and yawned. Then she came down on her heels and looked at us.

"Why are you two holding hands?" she said.

We all looked around.

My friend, hastily, jerked his hand back and mumbled: "Sorry."

He looked at his wife, blushed, and told all of us: "It just happened. I had no idea."

I leaned over and surveyed the skin of my hand. I could still see the traces of his fingers, the alternating of red and white after a long grip.

Then I looked up at them. But I no longer had much to say.

■ □ ■ □ ■

MY WIFE LOVES CATS

MY WIFE LOVES CATS.

A completely simple sentence that conceals a bottomless gulf of misunderstanding.

"But, if I remain indifferent to your love for syntax," says my wife, "why should my love for cats disturb you?"

During the afternoon, in countless little bowls, she prepares feline delicacies: entrails, liver, porridges and puddings, chicken feet, kidneys, bologna, milk. Then down she goes to the yard, rattling the heaping little pots and pans, the knocking of her clogs echoing in the stairwell. I watch from the terrace as she pours each dish into a particular container. Smaller bowls for the bigger cats; larger ones for several cats; milk in countless saucers. She straightens up, wipes her hands on her apron, and calls them.

I may not know what love is, but I do know magic. Magic is the way countless cats appear that instant, the way she guides them, urges their noses into the bowls, how she strokes their arching backs, how their tails fluff, how they claw up her trouser legs.

I go back into the kitchen, circle through the empty apartment. I go over to a cupboard, open it, peer inside to see what's there.

When my wife comes back from the yard, she'll ask me what I want for dinner. I'll tell her. We'll dine in silence. I will try in vain to find a cat's hair in my food, on the sheet, on her blouse, in the bread; at the end she'll serve dessert: vanilla pudding.

I adore vanilla.

Once my wife said, "Hatred distances a person from nature; love returns you to the cradle of the universe."

What she meant to say was that a person who loves lives in harmony with the rhythms of the world: day for him is day, night is night. He opens his eyes in the morning, in the evening he closes them.

She, of course, is horrified by such explanations. She says, "If words can't say what they tell us, then what are words for?"

Indeed, what are words for?

I hear the echo of her clogs: she is coming back. I sit back down in my place. Let her find me the way I was when she left me.

But at night while I lie there awake and she sleeps, I sometimes hear how she sighs. I lean over her, and though the light is weak, I see her nose quivering, her upper lip curling and pulling back, and she exposes the hidden white of her teeth, and I know—my wife is dreaming of a mouse.

■ □ ■ □ ■

STUDIO APARTMENT

EACH OF US HAS HIS OWN FORMULA TO FEND OFF LONELINESS. Mine is simple: an inch or so of cheap *vinjak,* the television on, salted pretzel sticks in a bowl on the table. Then slippers, soft, which don't pinch the toes.

Vinjak is the worst of all drinks, a lethal beverage. They say that if you leave an animal's guts soaking in Coca-Cola in a closed container for a few hours, they will disintegrate: the chemicals, sugar, and carbohydrates eat them away. I don't know if anyone has tried the same experiment, if you can call that an experiment, with cheap *vinjak,* but I am convinced that the result would be even better. Meaning: worse.

However, if what you have to drink is *vinjak,* then there is no point in fooling yourself that you are drinking French cognac. A person's fancy may be lively, but a person's body knows what it learns. You can't forge a taste.

Loneliness, for example. No one likes being alone, I'll agree to that. But the mistake many make—wanting not to be alone when they are alone—is the product of their fancy. The body is not angered by being alone; loneliness doesn't bother it, and it will be entirely satisfied regardless of whether it is in this or that corner. Whoever does not wish to be alone in his loneliness is destroying his body as alcohol destroys the liver. The soul is the Coca-Cola in which the body floats.

When I am alone, therefore, I know that I am alone, and that is all. I go slowly to the cupboard, open the liquor cabinet, pour myself an inch or so of *vinjak,* and sit down. I have already turned on the television, put on my slippers, run my fingers through my hair. The *vinjak* has a revolting taste. One day, I think, my tongue will blister from it.

My apartment is small—a one-room box on the next-to-last floor of an apartment building. When I sit in my armchair and stretch out my hand, I touch the wall. The wall is covered with wallpaper. Under my fingers, under the tips of my fingers, the wallpaper discloses the rough geography of its surface. After the fourth or fifth glass of *vinjak,* while the television is still on, I close my eyes and submit to the geography of my wallpaper. Later, when I open them, I see the glaring white screen, something remote from any geography.

The kitchen is a part of the antechamber. The bathroom is shabby. Once, at some girl's, I stood in the bathroom, which was covered from floor to ceiling with blue tiles. The floor was covered with blue tiles; the ceiling, too. There was a drawing of the sun, in some sort of color, in the corner. On the walls, about chest height, floated white clouds. The girl came with me into the bathroom while I was still standing on the blue tiles in the middle and asked me: "Aren't you going to take your clothes off?"

I turned and stared at her. She was already naked. "I should take my clothes off?" I asked.

She smiled. "I've never yet seen someone take a bath with his clothes on," she said.

I answered: "Live and learn."

She knelt, plugged the drain, and began to run the water. I undid my pants, and they dropped to my ankles. The girl turned and pushed her hair back from her forehead. She licked her lips and took it in her wide-open mouth. One of the clouds, I noticed, wasn't quite done.

The other mistake people make is the window. When they are alone, they perch by windows like migrating birds on telegraph wires. I never look out, I never move the curtain. A person is not an actor worrying how many people will attend his performance. A person who is alone must not look out or in; that is why the television is on in my room. Its scenes are powerful enough to draw your attention and weak enough to leave one room to think. Even when I close my eyes, when I submit to the geography of my wallpaper, I don't create any images inside me. I sink, empty, into the blessing of emptiness.

After the next glass, a total of three inches of *vinjak,* I take one salted pretzel stick. I nibble it slowly, bit by bit. First I lick the bigger lumps of salt off, then I squeeze it between my front teeth and break off a segment of a certain length. My rhythm is slow. Sometimes a single pretzel stick remains in my hand until the end of the evening's broadcast. Sometimes I empty out the bowl before the late news. But the rhythm remains the same because it is not tied to the flow of time.

Later, when the evening's television ends and the screen goes white, I get up and make my bed—the sheet, pillow, quilt. I turn off the light and get undressed in the dark. I shuffle over to the television and push the button. Although the bright glare goes out at once, the screen stays lit. I lie in bed, I watch the dying gleam and try to fall asleep in harmony with its vanishing. I close my eyes and peer through my eyelashes. Sometimes I do fall asleep at the same time. Most often, however, I must pretend. I pretend to sleep, squeeze my eyes shut, but I feel my eyelids twitch.

A few nights ago, maybe it was on Wednesday, for the first time in memory—though how reliable that is I don't know—I started and woke up. I opened my eyes wide and put my left cheek on the pillow. The television was dead. The window was staring straight into black sky. The bowl with salted pretzel sticks was precariously near the edge of the coffee table. The glass was standing in some sort of shadow. I couldn't see my slippers, but I knew where they were. I knew that the right one was leaning a little over the left, and that the left was nudging both socks. I couldn't see the socks either. I saw the curtain, I saw the wooden camel on top of the television set, I saw the place on the edge of the armchair I always touched with my little finger.

I didn't know why I'd woken.

Then the doorbell rang again.

I turned my head and lowered my right cheek onto the fabric of the pillowcase. The raised design on the wallpaper cast tiny shadows on uninhabited valleys. The pillow corner loomed high above all of us. I wondered whether perhaps I ought to get up and turn on the TV. Perhaps as the white glare was subsiding I'd be able to drop off to sleep again.

The doorbell rang a third time.

■ □ ■ □ ■

THE WALL

ONCE, LONG AGO, I WAS IN KENYA, OR WAS IT TANGANYIKA, I can't remember anymore. All I remember is a wall in front of which I stood, facing it, for ages. Out of the corner of my left eye I saw a stain that was certainly quite large, that probably covered the whole wall except the part in front of which I stood. Behind me, right nearby, but pretty far off, too, African feet pattered by, heavy, slow, without stopping. As far as the Africans were concerned, white men were already crazy enough to choose to be white men; that a white man was standing there and staring at some wall, while behind his back was Nairobi—if it was Nairobi—teeming with life, could only be proof that there was no end to the craziness. I knew they were thinking that, and my back knew it.

My wife, however, knew nothing. When I tried to explain to her how I *loved* black people, that there was nothing erotic in it, that I loved *only* the fact that they exist, their fragile, slow-moving ways, she told me I was queer. She said: You are queer. If you start talking to me one more time about their beauty, about their round little bottoms, I will leave you. Is that clear?

It sure is, though I had never spoken to her about the beauty of those round bottoms. Maybe I'd written something to her in some letter, if we knew each other back then, and if I wrote to her. If I did write to her, then that was before postcards. I don't believe that I would have written on a postcard about the beauty of African bottoms, unless the postcard showed strapping exemplars of some scantily clad tribe, Bantu or Masai or Pygmy. In that case I can't swear to it.

Once a week, usually on Saturdays, we went for lunch at my mother-in-law's. We sat in the growing dusk in the dining room and ate cold cuts. My wife would drink beer, her mother would drink mineral water, and I would drink white wine. After lunch, while the two of them were clearing the table, I would leaf through trashy weeklies in search of articles on Africa. Just in case, I'd keep one finger ready on the page where celebrities described their homes. If my wife came into the room, I'd flip to that page and start in on a description of the bed Vera Čukić, some movie star, used to sleep in. If her mother came in, I wouldn't go overboard; she understood my need to love the exotic.

Then we'd have coffee from fragile cups made of cobalt. Usually in silence. My wife occasionally glanced at her watch, at the clock on the wall, and at the large grandfather clock that stood on the floor and almost reached the ceiling and that didn't work. After that she'd usually say that she found it confusing, the stationary time, that frozen moment of eternity, and she'd ask whether it might be possible to repair that clock.

Her mother would turn her head, and I could see how the cobalt was trembling in her hand. No one does that sort of work anymore, she'd say. All the repairmen, she'd say, who knew how to have died. And the ones who are still alive, their hands shake. Then she'd stare at her hands. Like mine, she'd say.

Although I liked my wife's comment about stationary time, and although I sympathized with the contradictory comment her mother made about its transitoriness, I would do nothing. First of all, I was sitting facing the monster, myself paralyzed, just as I'd stood before the wall in Kenya, if it was Kenya. And secondly, time didn't interest me. Whoever was interested in time was living in time; those who didn't find time interesting lived outside of it. Time is an imposed category of human existence, if I dare be so explicit.

In the end we still needed to walk home. On our way home this last time, my wife slipped, and apparently she twisted her ankle. In the evening her ankle swelled up so much that I had to throw up. I went into the bathroom and stuck first my index finger, then my middle finger, deep into my esophagus. My esophagus said to me, "Your finger is here," but nothing came from my stomach. Leaning over the toilet bowl, I closed my eyes and felt the stench of ammonia. The proximity of things, the proximity of sensory stimuli, proximity in general, was what stirred in me the memory of the wall, and it seemed that I had never been closer to it.

She went to the doctor, and got a soft cast and a recommendation that she stay in bed a few days. Yesterday I peeked and saw that her ankle had shrunk so much that we could talk again. I asked her whether she needed anything. She said she'd like to drink a cup of tea or coffee, if I'd be willing to make some. I made some coffee.

"Despite it all," she said, "I like it when I talk with you. I like to hear your voice." She put down her cup and stared at me. "I think I couldn't live in silence."

I swallowed the last swig of coffee and crunched my teeth on a couple of bigger coffee grains.

"The part of town where we used to live," she went on, "it is so quiet there. When my parents went out, while father was still alive, I used to stay in bed and listen to the silence. Black furniture, like the kind we had, has a depth to it in which all sorts of things can appear."

I nodded.

"I don't know if you've experienced it," she said and left her cup on the table, "but while I lay there in the dark, in the silence, the curtains at the windows used to swing all by themselves. I could tell myself it's the air currents, the room is cooling, everything occurs according to set laws, but was that of any help to me?"

"No," I said.

"I held a hand between my legs," she said. "That way I felt safer." She stared at me again. "I don't know why I'm telling you this, I don't know whether you'll be able to see what I want to tell you, but down there, under my hand, there was something living that gave me back my courage, living and warm. It occurred to me that maybe the heart, if a person could reach it, would leave the same feeling on one's palm." She fell silent.

I coughed to clear my throat. "When I was in Africa," I said, and knew I'd made a mistake.

"You creep," she said, "you are one ordinary creep is what you are."

I got up and looked straight ahead. I saw a crack that went from the chandelier hook to some corner of the room, and I knew that one of these days, when the time came, all of it would break.

My wife, frowning, crossed her hands on her chest.

I said: "I have been sitting here for hours and listening to how you masturbated when you were little, and how now you are trying to attribute it to some higher goal, and when I try to tell you something that is really *me,* you spit in my face."

She didn't even look at me.

I said: "All I wanted was to tell you something that went with *your* story about silence, that's all."

She closed her eyes.

I said: "I only wanted to tell you how once, in the very heart of some African countryside, late at night, I got out of a car in the middle of some road and stepped out into the scruffy grass. What I heard then, that is what I wanted to tell you, and I didn't hear a thing, that, for me, was silence.

As if I'd been down among corals on the ocean floor. When I came back to the car and sat next to the tiny driver, I saw his wrist on the gearshift and knew the silence hidden in that black wrist."

She opened her eyes and shut them again.

I said: "Your problem is that you see in the world only what you are prepared to give it. For you there is only what you know. What you don't know, like the silence of that black wrist, is dead for you, it means nothing."

Finally she spoke. She said: "Don't force me to tell you what you don't want to hear."

"I know," I said. "I know what you attribute my love for that original blackness to, and I know how wrong you are. All of English literature, for instance, is based on that same love. If you don't understand that love, you can't understand the words that describe it. Joseph Conrad," I said and raised my forefinger. Then I raised my middle finger: "Graham Greene," I said. "Doris Lessing," I said for the third finger; "George Finchley," I fabricated for my little finger. "V. S. Naipul," I said for my thumb.

She said nothing. She weighed the words she would say to me, and by the length of her silence I knew how far we'd gone. She said: "And Charles Dickens?"

I sat, got up, sat again, got up again. She watched my movements with suspicion. She knew that now she was ahead of me on the route we had chosen, and she was afraid of a nasty blow to the back. I took her coffee cup, I took mine, and I put all of the things on the serving tray and went into the kitchen. While I was walking, her face shimmered in front of me, but when I'd gotten into the shadows of the hallway, the lines of her face merged with the curves on the wall in Nairobi, if it was Nairobi. In the sink there were still dirty dishes, but I washed only our cups and rinsed out the Turkish coffee pot. When I came back into the room, she was sleeping, or pretending to sleep—it seemed to me that she was pretending. Whatever the case, that stopped me. I stood like that, in the middle of the room, or maybe a little closer to the corner, and she lay on the couch. There was no sound. I listened in the room, but it was the same as if I had been in Kenya, in Zambia, in the Congo. I wanted to tell her that in life we have no choice, that we get only what we deserve, and that the only questions are whether we can improve ourselves alone or with the help of someone else, whether what we get will be a faithful reflection of our merits or will we live in disharmony and get much less than our due. I wanted, in the same way, to tell her that all this can be done in a terribly complicated, tangled manner, but that it can also be expressed in much simpler terms. I wanted to tell her that there is a formula for simplicity which states: Love comes to those who give. No one, you see, has ever been left without love, no one who ever gave unstintingly. But the ones who are only looking for love—I wanted to tell her that, too—they don't get anything. It's time, I wanted to tell her, for you to put that hand away; it's time to pull it out from below, from between your legs, and look for the place where your heart really is. That doesn't mean, I wanted to tell her, that I know where that place is or that I know what the human heart is at all, but it means that I feel something I still can't express and that I am longing for someone who would stand by my side in that scruffy African grass, there where silence is silent. When I moved, when I got into the car lit by the phantasmal light of the African night and gave myself over to the fragile beauty of that black wrist, I left myself on that same spot, in that same messy grass, through which snakes, spiders, and scorpions may have been crawling toward me, if there are scorpions in Kenya, and if that was Kenya. Who cares? That place where I stood, that's where I am today, and here where I'm standing I will stay, even when I start to move, even when I have moved across the room on my tiptoes in vain on the treacherous parquet floor, closer to and farther from my wife, who is sleeping over there, drowned between her firmly glued halves that no one ever, anywhere, is going to pry apart.

■ □ ■ □ ■

WORDS ARE SOMETHING ELSE

"SURE," SAID THE GIRL, "WHATEVER."

She pressed the receiver firmly to her ear, but couldn't hear anything. Was all this happening to someone else? she wondered. A moment later, with an almost fearful glance, she noticed a drop of perspiration suspended from her eyebrow. Across the room, behind her back, grew a cactus she had been taking care of for fourteen years.

"Are you there?" said a man's voice.

"Yes," said the girl, "I'm here."

The receiver was hung up in some unknown apartment.

The girl looked at *her* receiver, then with her arm wiped the sweat from her forehead. The curves of the Bakelite passed by her face like a stranger down a dark street.

She went into the kitchen. Her mother was knitting by the window. The transistor radio was not on, and the girl, who expected the transistor to be playing, felt she'd been cheated.

Her mother said, "In just a bit the cap will be done."

The girl went over and peered among her fingers.

"Who's it for?" she asked.

"No one in particular," answered her mother.

In the yard, under a weeping willow, there were two trash cans.

“He left me,” said the daughter. “We’ve just talked.”

Her mother raised her hand as if planning to pull the cap onto her head. She said, “That always happens.”

The girl moved toward a corner of the kitchen. She strode briskly and believed that she would not be able to stop herself.

“And besides,” said her mother, “if it happened like that, that means that it was meant to be.”

The girl turned. She felt like she was falling, but instead she touched the refrigerator. “I don’t care for the way he told me,” she said.

“How did he tell you?” asked her mother.

“In two sentences,” answered the girl.

“Could have done it in one,” said the mother.

The girl ran her finger along one of the letters on the refrigerator door. She didn’t know which letter it was, however, and would rather have traced a number. The number four, perhaps. Or the number five.

“He could have said nothing,” said the mother. She raised the cap again and looked at it against the light.

“Don’t be mean,” said the girl.

Her mother’s lips moved but she didn’t speak. She returned the cap to her lap and began to poke around in the basket with knitting wool.

“Who are you knitting the cap for?” asked the girl.

“I told you already,” said the mother. “No one in particular.”

“Sometimes,” said the girl, she placed her hand on the metal corner, “sometimes I wish I were dead. Sometimes I wish I’d never been born. I’d be better off if I were one of those blind cave salamanders in endless darkness than . . . ” She stopped; she couldn’t think of a thing.

Her mother lifted up several balls of wool. “What color should I use,” she asked, “to make the pom-pom?”

The girl came over with that same rapid stride. When she stopped, one part of her kept going. She saw how a gray-haired man went over to the trash cans and dumped trash into them. She ran a finger over all the balls of wool. The man backed away from the trash cans, then he went over to them again and pushed the lid on more firmly. "Take this one," said the girl, but when she'd turned, her mother had already left the kitchen.

"There is something else I haven't told you," said the girl when her mother came back. She went on standing by the window. Her left hand was curved around her neck while her right pressed the elbow of her left arm.

"Then don't," said her mother. She brought the finished pom-pom to her nose and sniffed it. She said, "This wool smells of tobacco." Then she stared at the girl. "Words won't bring him back," she said. "That's why I don't want to hear words. Say something else."

The girl shook her head. "That's not what I meant," she meant to say.

"Silence is stronger than any words," said her mother.

"That's not what I meant," said the girl.

"When you make a cap," her mother went on, "you have to put a pom-pom on the top. A cap without a pom-pom is like a baseball cap without a brim."

"What are you," asked the girl, "some Chinese wise man?"

"I make caps," answered her mother, "and what do you do?"

The girl sniffled. She pursed her lips and touched her tongue to a cavity in her tooth, which was growing with every passing day.

"If someone leaves you," said her mother, "then you sew a pom-pom on a cap, that's all. You don't fall onto the terrace like some plucked pigeon."

The girl said, "I understand." She turned around and watched the corner under the weeping willow.

"It is all pretty simple," said her mother. "Look!"

The girl turned. She could hear a snapping sound inside her, in her neck, in her tendons, and she thought: this is exactly how my head will fall off one day.

Her mother was holding a needle in her hand. "It is all pretty simple," she repeated. "If you want blood, you take it." She stabbed herself quickly in the index finger, then pressed her thumb to the ball of her finger. Crimson-colored blood appeared.

The girl looked her mother in the eyes.

"If you don't want blood," said the mother, "you wipe it up." She put her finger in her mouth and sucked on it. When she took it out, there was no blood.

"You didn't understand me," said the girl, "you didn't understand me at all." But she knew it was too late now.

When she left the kitchen she felt her knees shake. She stopped in front of a needlepoint tapestry depicting an idyllic landscape. A large wall clock behind her repeated its small-minded words. She began to move again, but only when she remembered that she'd been standing. She went into the bathroom and moistened her fingers under the water faucet from which water was always dripping. She looked into the mirror. She wanted to look at herself once more, but by then she was already in her room. She sat on the edge of the couch. If I had to choose between pants and a skirt, she thought, I'd choose pants. She was wearing a skirt. That's fine when it is summer or spring outside, or maybe fall, but when it's winter? It is good that I don't know which season it is now, she said to herself. Sitting there so still, she could hear the bed frame groan. She saw, also, a part of the sky through the window. The window was small and hard to open. Once long ago the girl had feared she'd choke if the window were open; later she feared she'd get sick if it didn't stay shut tight. Now she didn't care. She crossed her legs and considered her knees. She remembered the mirror she kept in her purse, not so far away, within reach, but she didn't like to think about distance in any way, shape, or form. She touched her knee with one and then with the other palm. She wanted to think about nothing, but she kept thinking about how she wanted to think about nothing. She got up. She sat down. She noticed a part of her face on some smooth surface. She is right, she thought, words won't bring him back. Words are something else.

■ □ ■ □ ■

MY WIFE SOFTLY SOBS

WHEN I CLIMBED UP TO THE FIRST MESA IN THE HOPI INDIAN reservation, I saw the end of the world.

When I came to the little place called Window Rock, I fell in love with a waitress, a short Navajo Indian woman who put the bowl of lamb stew down in front of me.

When I peered into Canyon de Chelly, I ached to spend the rest of my life there.

When I told all this to my wife, she asked: "Was the Indian woman fat?"

When I tried to explain to her that I did not feel like an outsider among the Indians, as Hans Mayer would put it, but instead like someone who, aside from skin color, was akin to them, she merely shrugged.

When I stubbornly repeated that Indians are actually New World Jews, my wife raised her eyebrows, stopped knitting, and put both hands on the table.

When I developed the rolls of film I had brought back from the trip, she studied them for a long time, concentrating on the photographed faces, regardless of whether they were blurred or in focus, close-ups or just a detail in a panoramic shot.

When, after I came home, I first had a dream about walking through the lands of the Navajo Indians, my wife woke me up and told me I'd been whinnying like a horse.

When we dined by candlelight a few days later, flickering

shadows moved across her face like clouds over the Grand Canyon.

When I told her about the myths of the Hopi Indians, she fell asleep just as I, as one of the gods of war, was leading the entire people out from the underworld in Arizona, where Masau'u, god of death, was waiting for us and showed us how to plant corn.

When she woke up, her face was creased with wrinkles, makeup had smeared over her eyelids.

When I reached the end of the town of Walpi, where the cliff of the first mesa drops vertically to the plain, I thought it might be simple to fly. I turned, thrilled, and saw my guide, a stout Hopi Indian woman, dozing in the treacherous rays of the sun.

Whenever you'd rather not be alone, you are; when you want to share something, you see that all the divvying up has gone on without you.

When I drew my wife's attention to the belief of several Navajo Indians that the first man and first woman were made of two ears of corn, night came rushing in the open window, the branches bent under gusts of wind, stars raced before frenzied clouds; my wife got up and went to the window, and the first sheets of rain coursed down her cheeks.

When I went into a hall crowded with Navajo Indians at Window Rock, I felt that, despite my best intentions, I was rather different; my white skin shone traitorously among the calm, ruddy faces. If I could have, I would have instantly changed myself into the turquoise pin on the leather jacket worn by an old Indian woman; only things can know what eludes people.

"When will you stop living your life as someone else?" asked my wife, and wearily leaned her forehead on her hand. "When will you be you and not someone else? When will you write a real story?"

When I started explaining that the essence of a story, and therefore its rightness or wrongness, is determined by the person who writes it, not the reader, and so by no means . . . she dismissed this curtly.

"When will you grow up?" she asks. "Life is not just listing facts or painting a picture; a person is supposed to lunge into life as into some deep whirlpool. When I'm reading, I want to feel like my lungs are about to burst because I'm out of breath, and at the end of the story, as I come up for air, my eyes are open wide with a new sense of insight into the order of all things. Do you understand, do you get it?"

When I emphasize that my story records the precise moment of *my* coming up for air, that after visiting the Navajo and Hopi Indian tribes I am no longer the same person, which means that the order of things in me and in the world has changed irreversibly, she refuses to discuss it further.

When I emphasize that my story imitates the simple rhythm of Indian songs, in which, aside from the flute, drums, and rattles, there are no other instruments . . .

When I say that this world exists only so that all the people in it can find places of their own . . .

When I describe the confrontation of traditions and the modern world among the Navajo Indians, in which I recognized the fits and starts of my own Jewish identity . . .

When my wife . . .

When I . . .

When the great flood ended, as the Lakota and the Pawnee believe, the Creator placed the buffalo in the northern lands and instructed it to stay the waters. The buffalo is still there, but each year it loses one of its hairs; when all its hairs are gone one day, the world will be flooded again. I see how it looks; I see myself, I see my wife, I see the buffalo, nearly hairless, as it shivers, assailed by gusts of the north wind. I see the mud we will soon be wading through in our frantic attempt to reach the south. Then a large wave will separate us, my wife will become a scream, the buffalo above our heads will twist skyward, and then everything will be silence, all beginning and nothing ending, only the eagles of Indian souls circling ever upward, higher and higher, finally free—which we, of course, will never be.

When I stop talking, this is what I hear: my wife softly sobs.

■ □ ■ □ ■

THE CLOAK

"YOU DON'T WRITE STORIES ABOUT ME ANYMORE," MY WIFE says sadly.

I look at her; everything has left its mark: the children, illness, life, war, death.

"I don't tell stories anymore," I say.

The sentence doesn't comfort her. She continues to move, slowly, with difficulty, as if she is pushing something in front of her. That was the way she moved while she was pregnant, when I put my hand, or an ear, to her stomach to feel the movement, or listen to the new heartbeat. Her stomach glowed white in the dark, and my hand neared it like a spaceship, stopping sometimes just above the skin, at the edge of warmth.

Around that time, I remember, I pulled off a sweet deal: for a relatively small sum I bought a hundred grams of hashish. Forty I sold, covered most of my investment, gave ten away to friends, and was left with a neat fifty, a big hunk of shit. It wasn't only me left; *we were left*. Our apartment—the old apartment, not where we live now, which is still new, cold, unaccustomed to people, but that old place—gave off a cloying odor, soft as only hash can be soft, yet at the same time harsh, precise, if you can say something like that about an odor. We got stoned together in front of the television set. Although she hadn't been smoking while she was pregnant, my wife did not refuse to take the proffered joint. She held it with her thumb and forefinger and took two long tokes, always two.

This infuriated her friend, Elizabeta. She came upon us one afternoon when we were smoking. I rolled a large joint of three brightly colored papers. In fact, each was the flag of some country, from Africa, Europe, Asia.

"Don't you realize what that does to babies?" Elizabeta fumed. She took the joint from my wife, cupped her hand around it, and took a long drag.

"No, I don't," my wife said, and laughed.

Maybe she shouldn't have laughed.

"There is no reliable medical evidence," she went on, "that cannabis causes anomalies of any sort. After all, doesn't the father expose the child to it, too, with his seed?"

Elizabeta didn't like the word "seed." As if the child were a plant, she said.

"Corn," said my wife. She had just been reading North American Indian myths in which corn sprung majestically from the hair of a deer, a cat's whiskers, and buffalo tracks.

Elizabeta closed her eyes and pursed her lips.

I thought how she was probably imagining an ear of corn, how she was probably counting the kernels.

Suddenly it got dark. The air became sticky and dense. Sweat beaded on Elizabeta's upper lip. Her forehead was dry. Like my wife's. She gave me back the joint. My hit singed the remains of the Swedish flag.

"Once in a TV movie," my wife said, "instead of a flag, stars were burning on a joint."

The first thunderclap banged, hail pelted the aluminum roof on the balcony. Elizabeta didn't open her eyes. Sparrows, pigeons, two turtledoves huddled under the eaves of the building across the way. A black shape might have been a crow.

"It's moving," my wife said, and touched her hip.

Elizabeta smiled.

"We should sit here, all of us," I said, "with eyes closed while ice envelops the planet."

"Ice brings back the light," said Elizabeta. "Ice does not conquer."

"What is this," my wife said, "a short story or an exercise in metaphysics?"

"Close your eyes," I said, "and you'll see."

She closed them.

"What now?" asked my wife.

"Shush," said Elizabeta, "someone is still looking."

"Is not," I lied.

"Is too," said Elizabeta, "He's looking and filching the light from the ice."

"From the sky," said my wife.

"Who cares?" said Elizabeta. "Light is light, and that won't change."

When I finally did close my eyes, I saw everything: the light, a throne, a hand, a touch. I didn't actually see the touch; I felt on my cheek something like a gentle pinprick, a pinch of frost, pine needles. I could hear how someone was breathing, how someone was walking, how someone was taking a seat, how someone was standing. Actually, there were no sounds. I saw as if I were looking with my ears, as if I were listening with the skin on my face. Elizabeta moved. My wife moaned. The cuckoo sang: Coo-coo. The storm thundered around our building like cavalry. The tenants called to each other from their balconies. The window glass rattled. Everything got shorter, everything grew longer. The joint worked its way to my lips. Feet lifted from the floor. Or the floor stretched away from my feet. Or the soles of my feet got thicker. Names fled from things. Someone mentioned the price of cooking oil. That person said: The value of cooking oil drops daily. Newspapers rustled. The refrigerator rumbled in the corner. The flower in the pot sighed, exhausted with thirst. It longed to flaunt itself; feeble, it fluttered its leaves. The manual was unrelenting: one must cross the great water by rowboat, ship, or on foot. Stone settled into the void as if it had always been waiting precisely in the middle of the room. This surely must have been written somewhere. For instance, the postman has a mustache. For instance, smoke is cold. For instance, a heart must stop sooner or later. Like shadows in a grove of trees which melt into the spreading twilight.

And then everything grew still.

We sat in the silence and waited.

Someone tiptoed down the stairs like a fugitive.

"Now I know," said my wife, "beauty is a cloak on the shoulders of the world."

She got up and went to the window, or we imagined that she did. She could have gotten up and gone over to Elizabeta to bury her face in her hair, too. She could have gotten up to sit down. I did not open my eyes. The door creaked, keys jangled, the cuckoo said nothing. For dinner, later, we ate French toast. My wife put a knife and fork in my hands, crossed them, and ordered me to cut. So I cut.

Now she expects me to find words to express what she cannot say herself. As if words are a human body that can be bent any which way, moving from crouch to standing without bringing into question the muscles' smoothness, the firmness of the bones, the soul's well-being.

I look at her. Everything has left its mark: illness, the children, war, life, death.

"The world," I say, "has dropped its cloak and is dragging it behind, like a child who drags an apron around after playing at the sink."

She shakes her head. It rings no bells. Memory, after all, is only personal property, something never owned in common. Elizabeta has long since stopped coming to visit. My wife has stopped smoking. The child is a girl whose absences from the house are longer than the time she spends here. Sometimes I imagine the boys she is sleeping with. They have smooth skin, refined hands, knobby knees; she rests her head on their hairy chests and with her lips she brushes their hard collarbones. This tickles the boys and they flinch, which she takes as an invitation so she grabs them by the hips. The boys grumble, they'd rather sleep. My daughter stretches out her hand, clicks off the light, and wedges her leg between their thighs.

That dark is the same as the darkness behind my eyelids.

Everything else is different.

PART III

■ □ ■ □ ■

THE ESSAY

ON THURSDAY IN THE EVENING, OR RATHER, LATE THAT night, around 11:15, just when I was getting ready, flicking on the light to walk into the kitchen, I was attacked by two cockroaches. One of them moved from the corner on my right, aiming, obviously, to assault my unprotected flank, while the other shoved aside the table and confronted me face to face. Luckily, their initial blows (which, I believe, were counting on my surprise and my lack of readiness) were not well gauged. I blocked the first and sidestepped the rest completely. Furthermore, taking advantage of a momentary lapse in caution from the cockroach on my right, I dealt it a powerful blow to the neck, and panting, it crumpled to my feet. The other attacker, surprised by the sudden turn things were taking (not, however, one so foreign to contemporary theater), lowered its legs and stepped back. It even seemed to me that I could see clear signs of alarm in its eyes. Without losing a moment, I leaned over and nabbed the stool that was by the pantry door, and, with a wild scream, I mashed the head of my opponent. The cockroach stumbled, leaned on the table, and keeled over, knocking over a vase with purple hyacinths as it went. Clear liquid sprayed every which way.

I heaved a sigh of relief. But, suddenly, I felt a wrenching jab to the foot. The first cockroach, stunned by my initial blow down on the concrete floor, had by now recovered, and it firmly latched its jaws on my knee, trying with all its force to bring me down. On the floor, I knew, on the floor I'd be a goner. Who has ever managed to overpower a cockroach on the floor? I tried to wrench free, but the cockroach was stronger. Resisting with its feet, it dragged me down. The sole remaining option was to think thoroughly about everything.

Good Lord, you may well exclaim, now he wants to think? In such a predicament?

But I ask you: What else could I do?

And I ask you: What would *you* have done in my place, in such a bind? You cannot deny I had tried everything. No? No. I tried to fight. I am not much of a fighter, even in my fights with people; I may have tussled three or four times, but only when I was a kid, and now: *cockroaches!* I did my level best. Wasn't one of the cockroaches lying under the table, its head mashed? And didn't I slug this other cockroach, the one dragging me downward at this very moment, in its jaws, into death? Did I not punch it in the neck? With a punch that knocked it flat? How could I possibly have known that it was in far better shape than your average cockroach accustomed to a carefree city existence? The other creatures of this species I had encountered until that instant were naturally much smaller and nowhere near as aggressive, timid even. Hadn't they all made short work of, if you'll pardon the French, getting the fuck out of there, hightailing it for the first hole or crack or—in their ignorance—into a shadow cast by a plate that hadn't been put away? Well, indeed. I mean, I guess a person always must be ready for all sorts of surprises in life. We must not permit ourselves to let down our guard even for a split second. Not a second. Or else.

There you see. What happened to me may serve as a warning to others. A model for what to avoid at all costs. Proof that in this century of industrialization, conflicting ideals, communication and the mass media, the human individual *must never* relax. For the cockroach in this story is actually a symbol of nature—nature we have, of course, ignored. It might just as well be a symbol of urbanization, newly laid plumbing, shoddy insulation, suburban neighborhoods thrown together too hastily, and so forth. Or, then again—I hope the critics will forgive me the liberty of literary fence-sitting—a symbol of tradition, dilapidated, once-sturdy houses and sloppily paved streets, clogged septic tanks, and linden trees, which still, with effort, manage to bloom. Or, a lack of faith in the future. Etc. Etc.

So what did you have in mind at the time?

Dated art forms.

In such a predicament?

Yes. The cockroach was dragging me to the floor. I staggered, braced myself against the wall, flailing with my arms all the while in a futile attempt to grab hold of something and keep from toppling over. But, while I was inching down the wall, my eyes shot to the window. I felt a sudden, irresistible urge to see the sky just one more time.

A feeling of imminent death?

If you prefer: yes.

And?

And then, at that moment (I hope you can see me glued to the wall, widespread but helpless arms, sinking straight into the jaws of an oh-so-traditional cockroach), I thought of the exhaustion of existing art forms. I saw it clear as day. Written out as if on a flashing neon sign. Red. Yellow. Garish.

Something specific?

Oh yes: specific. I was struck by the fact that in this situation—assuming, of course, that this was happening in a story or novella (a novel would go on too long)—I had only two options. First: I survive. Second: I do not survive. If the writer—we're still imagining that I am the hero of a story—were to opt for the first, then this scene would be followed by a slightly broader array of options for how to describe my salvation. For instance: *serendipity*—a glass globe breaks free, fortuitously, from the ceiling chandelier and with a horrible smash it kills the attacker; *necessity*—man is stronger than cockroach, i.e., his victory is essential, new characters are introduced, fighting brigades, peacekeeping forces, so forth; *allegory*—it was all a dream; *mythological phenomenology*—cockroach manages to drag man to floor, but man invokes primeval forces and rises again, and so it repeats (see Prometheus, Sisyphus, Hercules, Inanna, Absalom); *symbolism*—see the above; and a whole series of other, more or less happily chosen ways out. The second version: I do not survive, generally implying greater social thrust. The author is labeled as harboring nihilistic leanings, the establishment and big names level stinging critiques, they call upon the author to shoulder responsibility, "others of the same ilk" are branded, and excommunication is brandished (regardless of one's faith) by the Catholic Church.

But what happened, really?

Braced, as I was, against the wall and suffering from sharp pain in the realm of my knees, slipping downward, helplessly flailing my arms, meanwhile looking out the window, my hand suddenly banged into the lock on the pantry door. Immediately thereafter my fingers closed on a cold, rough object. A key! That rusty and blackened key we never used! A solution! Salvation! Art must overcome its timeworn constraints! Polysemantic it must be! It must strive for synthesis, condensation! Before my very eyes flashed visions of tomorrow. Man will soon have to listen, watch, touch, and feel, all at once. Art must fuse! As one! With these thoughts I grabbed the key and flung myself, with renewed vigor, on the merciless enemy. And while we rolled about the floor with groans and shrieks, I began to hammer blows furiously on its conventional black shell. To the underbelly! To the flank! To the temples! To the heart! The heart! The heart! The cockroach sagged, and with effort I wriggled out from underneath. My clothing was stained with lymphatic ooze, but in my hands I still clutched my weapon. The key. The solution. My knees buckled.

Then I wondered: Had my parents heard any of this?

I went to the door and listened. Nothing. Surely they were sound asleep.

But. I was shaken at once by new fear. What if their silence meant that something had befallen them? A prowler while I was out? Burglars attacking? A natural disaster? Or, God help us . . .

I rushed into the room. When there . . . look!

Father and Mother, in each other's arms (Father wearing a Panama hat, in his slippers with no socks; Mother in a long white floral-patterned nightgown, her hair up), were dancing the tango. In perfect silence. Now and then the parquet floor squeaked or they nudged the furniture. Antiques. They seemed oblivious of me. Mother, her head cocked to the side, stared off somewhere into romantic distance. Father, resting his head on her shoulder, danced with his eyes shut. I gasped with relief. Everything was fine, after all. They heard nothing in their soundless dancing. I could go back. But. Only then, when their faces shone in the pale glow of the kitchen table lamp, did tears gleam on Father's cheeks. Crystals in fractured colors. Rhomboids of inevitability. And Mother's hair, Mother's hair was pure gray. Pure gray. Father, I said. But, Mother. Their beds weren't even rumpled. My God, I realized, they dance all night.

I tiptoed away and went back to the kitchen. The corpses of the cockroaches lay where I'd left them: one under the table, the other by the stove. I brought the dustpan and brush in from the terrace and carefully swept them up. I took care not to leave behind a single chunk of their piecemeal bodies. Probably, thanks to the benefit of bountiful and regular nutrition, their size had outstripped the dimensions of their species. I measured them with a tailor's tape: 14 and 12.1 centimeters. Good Lord! I tossed them into the trash.

Of course, the sight of their crushed bodies stilled my appetite. I was not hungry. In my mouth I had—to express myself colorfully—the acrid taste of death. I opened a bottle of peach juice and gulped it down out there on the balcony. It was cool outside. The wind brushed my face, and the nearest poplars rustled. There were no stars in the sky.

I locked the door, put out the lights, and started to get ready for bed. From my parents' bedroom I could hear their steady breathing. Of late, drained by work and life, they sleep deeper and deeper, and rarely notice my late arrival. They leave me dinner on the kitchen table, and my bed made.

I pulled on pajamas and slipped under the covers. Shadows flitted along the walls from late-night cars; in the room, which soon grew chilly, the warmed objects crackled. The cuckoo sang "cuckoo." Every tradition, I thought, my eyes closing, sooner or later becomes the most ponderous of burdens, and every instance of its violation the artist's obligation. The avant-garde must be short-lived; there is no such thing as a scream without end.

And so, lightly, I drifted off to sleep.

■ □ ■ □ ■

WHAT DOES THAT PROVE?

SEVERAL TIMES A WEEK—THREE OR FOUR, NOT MORE, BUT never less—I lean over slowly and peer under the bed. "Slowly," in this case, is a handy word, but inadequate to describe the way in which I lean, due to the fact that the way, in the sense I have in mind, is a determinant for the time I need to lean down, three or four times a week, and peer under the bed. Last time, for example, I started to lean over before noon. I guess it must have been around eleven o'clock, probably closer to ten, certainly between ten and eleven, and I peered under the bed around five in the afternoon. At five in the afternoon the shadows are no longer crisp, and if one keeps in mind that my only window is a small one, a tiny window, really, on the slant of the roof, I am invariably surprised when I see how much you can see down there where by all counts you shouldn't be able to see anything, or almost nothing, at all. Straightening up, of course, straightening up goes much more rapidly. This is a movement I don't expect much from, a change that does not excite me. Perhaps it excited me once, but today, these days, these last few weeks, standing up has been an immutable fact, a necessity that changes nothing. Leaning down, however, that metaphoric descent from the heights, if I can refer to it as such, to the nether spheres, leaning is a process of unending wonder, unending awe at the bounty of the universe, and astonishment, of course, at the limitations of human beings. For while one's viewpoint—sometimes wobbly, sometimes steady—descends from the crack where two rafters join, over a stain supposedly left from wallpaper (as others claim, though not I; I don't believe there ever was wallpaper here), to the edge of the coverlet, for example, or over (or should I say through? therefore, through) that great void that could be above the bed, next to it, or anywhere, one comes to grasp (I am talking about myself again as if I am not here, but I am, indeed I am) that man has chosen the poorest of all existences, one that relies upon the rigidity, immutability, and magnitude of all things. However, when they once asked me why I lean over at all, I had no clue what to reply. I said something, mostly words. And what do you see down there? Shadows, first of all. Aren't there shadows above, too, aren't they everywhere? Are they? They are. What now? Am I supposed to ask something? We conversed while I was leaning over, while I was descending, in so many words, into those unheard-of depths, and I couldn't attend to the conversation. I was listening with only one ear, I haven't heard anything in the other ear for ages, left or right—one of the two in any case—and words elude me, words have been eluding me for some time. But when I straightened up, they were still leaning over. "What are you doing here?" I asked, appalled. They looked at how I was standing there, tall and strapping, I haven't used that word for ages, perhaps I fancied it wrongly, but whatever the case, and it would be best for it to be precisely as it is, they were startled. And what are *you* doing here? they asked me. I straightened up, I told them that I had straightened up. We know that, they said, but when? When what? When did you straighten up, how did you straighten up so fast, they asked, when here we are still leaning? An intriguing question; I had to think. Don't think, they said, answer us now. If you don't answer us, they said, we will sulk. What does that mean, "sulking"? I asked. They exchanged glances; if I hadn't been in the room they probably would have started whispering to each other. Fine, they said, we won't sulk, but you have to answer us, you can't abandon us like this, leaning. Will you lean over again? Do you want me to lean over again? We do. What time is it? Three, they said. Do you know, I said, do you know how long my leaning can take? We know. So? Hurry, hurry, they said. I hurried, but somewhere about halfway down, actually, just before halfway down rather than just after, earlier rather than later, I spotted a crack I had never noticed before. It had spread next to a tile, though some think it's wallpaper, it spread into a cluster of feelers, and each feeler had a little array of its own, and out of all those little feelers, all those fractures, three continued spreading further, and on one of the teeny cracks, so fine that there was no longer a word to describe them, I saw a bud, a tiny bud, which promised a new blossoming of cracks. I thought I might turn around, draw their attention to the subject of my attention, but what could I say to them, I wondered: how to tell them something that had no name, how to tell them something that officially doesn't even exist? To say to them: a bud blossoming with feelers? On the other hand, I had to hurry, they were waiting for me. I promised, I continued, I descended. I peered under the bed and turned. They had straightened up. What now? We couldn't wait for you, they said. Why? Well, look at the time! What time is it? Six-thirty. Six-thirty? I warned you, I said. We know, they said, but you stayed too long. Longer than you expected? Longer. How much longer? Much longer. And now what? Nothing, they shrugged. At roughly the same moment we all looked at my little window. It wasn't entirely dark outside yet. Maybe, maybe if I were to lean once more, if I were to get up and immediately begin to lean, perhaps I could peer under before all the shadows merge. No, I'm fooling myself. I can't make it before dark, though even in merging darkness there are nuances one should know, which not everyone knows. In that case, I said, this is the end of the day. What does that prove? they asked. What does that mean, "prove"?

I answered. They exchanged looks; if I hadn't been in the room they would probably have started whispering to each other. I wouldn't have been surprised to discover that they'd brought an encyclopedia. To prove, they said, means to confirm the truth. And a lie? I asked. They exchanged glances again, and if I hadn't been in the room, who knows, they might have called in someone else. Lies, too, they said. Then it doesn't matter which is which, I said, what matters is the proving. With that they agreed. But the end of the day, I said, cannot be the end of the night. They agreed with that, too. What does that prove? I asked. They exchanged looks again. Then they looked at me. Gotta go, they said. There's nothing I can do about that, if someone's got to go, he'll go, but if someone does not want to go, he won't; if someone wants to stay, he'll stay, if someone does not want to not stay, then what does that person do? As far as they were concerned, they left. I looked up, I looked down. I'm tired. I'd already peered under the bed twice. I did not, in practical terms, have a moment's respite. I discovered several new things regarding my wall, and regarding the system of the universe, and regarding interpersonal relations, and regarding new words. I learned several new words. I learned how cracks multiply, or blossom, but that is surely one and the same—all in all: an exhausting day. But still day. No, it's night. At night, as far as I can recall, at night I have never yet peered under the bed. I am tired, I needn't say so again, but that is why I'm anxious—where did that word come from?—that I might not make it, and if I start, now or presently, to lean, I probably wouldn't make it before dawn, and at dawn shadows are muted, and last only briefly, and perhaps at precisely the moment when I'd be passing the lower edge of the bed, perhaps precisely at that moment all shadows might vanish, and I would find myself in front of a vacuum about which I prefer not to talk, which reminds me of a pledge I once made long ago, to my mother or father or younger sister, that I would put a curtain up on the little window, a thick curtain of dense material, of opaque material, or with little holes, though plain paper, if I only had a few sheets of paper, would do, they'd do just fine. I have never been someone who could be trusted fully.

■ □ ■ □ ■

THE WRITER

AS HE SHUTS THE DOOR BEHIND HIM, THE WRITER PAUSES FOR several moments in the pitch black of the stairwell, thinks the writer. Then his hand rises to the switch—this is a long-practiced gesture and there is no room for error—and only a moment later light floods the scene. But the writer is not satisfied. It all happened too fast; he is more intrigued with a version that would unfold as follows: when the writer finds himself in the gloom of the hallway and lifts his hand toward the switch for the hall light, he realizes, aghast, that the switch is not where it should be. The writer probes the wall, first a bit above, then a bit below the place where the red switch used to be (apparently he remembers its color, too), but in vain. He inches forward, then back, patting—with both hands—the dusty wall surface, but he does not find what he's looking for. The writer fidgets with excitement in his chair. Tension, or, more precisely, the despair of the writer lost in the dark, is stirring him. Naturally the name of Robert Coover flashes through his mind; he remembers that he has read one—make it two!—of his stories structured in much the same way: In the first, a man turns out the light and moves toward his bed where his naked wife is lying, only to discover that the room is strange and that he cannot reach her. When he finally does, and when he starts to make love to her in the dark, the door swings open, police charge in, the light is switched on, and the man sees with disgust that his wife is dead, that she is already decomposing, etc. In the second story, a man—probably not the same man, though we are never told this in so many words—comes out of the bathroom, turns off the light, and he, too, goes over to his bed, but when he lies down and turns on his bedside lamp, he is aghast to see four or five people in bed with him, etc. All of this flashes through his (the writer's, naturally) mind much more quickly than it does for him to write or tell of it, so when we find ourselves at this point, the writer has already begun to pat the concrete floor of the landing, convinced that he must have experienced a change in perspective, that what was up is now down and vice versa, while the writer is still sitting in his chair. His excitement is apparent by now, and we would hardly be surprised to see sweat beading on his forehead. He, however, is interested in something else: Who is behind that door? Why did the writer come out into the hall in the first place? Why is all this happening? But aren't these questions he should be coming up with answers for? The writer, on the other hand, has decided to be reasonable: he straightens up in the pitch black, he runs the fingertips of his right hand along the wall, stretches his left hand sideways toward the bannister. His plan is simple. When he gets a grip on the bannister he will walk down the stairs and go out into the street. He has done just this countless times before: during blackouts, in his childhood, in the days when sneaking was required. As far as he can figure—in simple terms, for he was never too good at math—if he spreads his arms out straight but not too far, he knows precisely where the bannister is: when he pushes his right hand off from the wall and only slightly extends the fingers of his left hand, he will touch the bars on the ironwork railing. When he does precisely this, however, the writer touches nothing. Then, only an instant later, when he regains his balance on his right foot and stretches his right hand back to the wall, nothing is there. What had he been expecting, anyway? muses the writer. The writer does not respond. We can assume that the prose of Robert Coover is not unknown to him, either; literary influences spread with incredible speed. Does all this confirm that we can know nothing except for something someone knows already? The writer stops writing so he can muse on all the ramifications of these questions—which certainly does nothing to ease the plight of the writer stuck in pitch black who is beginning to feel as if he is losing his mind, slowly but surely. He can almost describe the sensation: as if something (his reason, presumably) is separating from him, but in such a way that he seems to grow more and more weightless. Perhaps total weight loss might help, he thinks: he'd rise up, bodiless, into the air, to the heights, and perhaps here, where he had least hoped for it, he might find the way out. We could all use a way out, thinks the writer. Each of us has found himself at his dead end, thinks the writer. Can a writer stop thinking like a writer? thinks the writer. The writer thinks this might be plausible. But would it be useful? Indeed. But we know something else. We know in advance the moral of the story that the writer and the writer will arrive at only much later. Folk wisdom has it: Do not open doors you don't know how to close. Or rather: Do not close the door before you turn on the hall light. Neither writer has considered this. The first one is still not thinking about it; the second would like to think about it, but he has lost his ability to reason. He stands in the dark like refuse, like a rock, like a snail. Perhaps the comparison with the snail is a bit strained. He breathes, he watches, his heart beats, his pulse pounds, he swallows his saliva, he has a stone in his kidney. What, of all this, applies to the snail? Nothing to speak of. Before he became what he is now, he contemplated writing a story about a writer who writes a story about a writer who no longer knows who, what, or where he is. Which places the first writer in a much more difficult fix, because he is no longer sure whether he is plunking away at the typewriter because he wants to or because someone else wants him to. The danger lies precisely in the fact that we can find ourselves in a hopeless situation by imagining someone else in a hopeless situation. Tenderness should be our primary quality, then generosity, and then mercy. Evil returns, others wiser than us have proven that, thinks the writer. He would now give everything in the world to run his finger through the darkness of the last few lines, sheets of paper, and printer's ink, to flip on the red switch. The light would blaze like a discovery; he would not claim it as his own. I would not claim the light as my own, thinks the writer. The writer in the dark thinks nothing. He is now a living corpse, a testimony to the lethal effects of prose upon its protagonists. If he could utter the word "light," he would feel the same as if he should say "apple," or "whipped cream," or "clothes hanger," or "the universe has no beginning and no end, instead all within it exists simultaneously in a single place and in a multitude of places." And so it goes: here today, gone tomorrow. The trick is to figure when today is and when tomorrow is; the simplest thing turns out to be the most complex. Such as those two steps, for example, which he is supposed to take from the apartment doorway to the place where the light switch for the stairwell light was. One false move gives rise to a whole story.

■ □ ■ □ ■

PLASTIC COMBS

ONE SUMMER DAY SHE TOLD ME TO LEAVE AND NOT COME back. She stood in the doorway, somewhat bulkier than usual, which I found particularly appealing, and said: Go away and don't come back. Good, I said, I'll go, but I asked whether I might not take my things with me. I had some things I thought I'd rather not give up. Sure, she said. She turned, and I saw how her powerful muscles bulged under her short sleeves, how her belly, under the chintz rhombs of her blouse, overflowed her taut underpants. Then I dedicated myself to my belongings. I took them in my hand one by one and weighed them, first on the right, then on the left palm. I weighed them all, their meaning, their sense, their place in my life, and their position in the general order of things, which is only another way of saying in the cosmos. The pile on the right side shrank, and the pile on the left side grew, and when I'd finished and touched the place between my legs, I found only a single needle, which I thought might come in handy, on the condition, of course, that I had some thread, too, which I didn't just then. I put the needle onto the left pile, too, stood up, brushed off my pants, straightened my shirt, and then I wondered what I'd do with the hat, on which palm should I put it? I put it on the right, then on the left, then on my head. I looked at it in the mirror, put it down on the table, and stepped back, squinting with one eye. I couldn't make up my mind. I had

had the hat for a long time, indeed, but did that mean a thing to the hat? Do things know as much about us as we know about them? I observed the hat but it did not respond. Meanwhile, she had come back. She'd combed her hair behind her ears and kept it in place with plastic combs; I had the impression she'd washed her face. I asked her about the hat. No, she said, she knew nothing about hats. Was it my hat? I asked. If the hat is all that matters, said she, why don't we speed this up, why don't you treat that hat as if it is yours? And what, I asked, if it isn't mine? Let's say it's yours, she said, for if you wear that hat, you'll begin to resemble Thomas Bernhard, and maybe someone else, but Thomas definitely. Good, I said, placed the hat on my head and left. I set out up hill. Soon it was apparent I'd been mistaken, that the hat was not mine after all, for it slid down my forehead, onto my ears, down my neck. I didn't get far, maybe a dozen meters, maybe more, maybe a bit less, and I was soaked in sweat. Who went around in the middle of summer wearing a hat? If my hands had been full, I might have added the hat to what I was carrying, but since they were empty, why should I clutter them up? I went back. She was standing on the threshold, hand on hip, locks of hair in her eyes. You should never trust plastic combs, I said. Why did you come back? she asked. So you could take off my hat, I said. And then you'll go? she asked. You just take it off, I said. She took hold of the rim, with her left hand on the right side and her right on the left, and yanked. The hat slipped, my hair rose with it, and at once I could feel a breeze. It was a summer breeze, sticky and thick, but it was a breeze. Hold onto it, I told her. She held onto the hat with the tips of her fingers, held it far away from her, like dirty diapers. I set out uphill again, but this time I walked with more spring in my step; I sweated, but all over; if a man always knew what was holding him back, he'd find it easier to free himself both of ballast and of self. I turned. She was still standing at the threshold. The hat was not visible, which could mean only one thing: she'd tossed it or kicked it away, which is something else again, and which I would have loved to see; I would have given anything to see how she kicked the hat, and how the hat, sodden with sweat, took lightly to the air and then plummeted to the depths. I, however, climbed to the heights. On both sides of the road there were open meadows, lawns, flowery fields. Bees hummed, flies buzzed, occasionally a bird would chirp. The peak was no longer far off; it never had been far, but I needed a bit more time, whether climbing or descending, and especially when I was going straight. At the top I missed the hat. The wind picked up, or perhaps I had come too close to it; in any case, it whistled around my ears, my wet shirt stuck to me, my trousers, too. Stuck-together blades of grass lashed at me like whips. When will you learn, I said to myself, that you should trust things the way you trust people? Now it was too late. I could have gone back, but I could not have opened that door anymore. It would not have opened for me at all; there's not a single one that will open for me, least of all the ones I most expect to. When things grow disappointed in someone, it is difficult to win back their trust. I shivered, looked at my shoes; I have had them for ages and have never doubted the fact that I own them. Then I looked around, left, then right, then left again, then right again, and who knows how long I would have spun back and forth like that if it hadn't been for hearing the call of a lark. What was a lark doing here? If there were larks, perhaps there were moles as well. Again I missed that hat: so wide-brimmed, I could have used it for hunting, for larks and moles, maybe even rabbits. I admonished myself again. Now I had no choice but to set out down the slope, and while the gravel squirmed under my feet, I tried to calm the shaking of my knees. The wind let up a bit, and I started sweating again. The slope began to undulate, the grass was thicker, and the valleys hid countless surprises. Somewhere about halfway along—only guesswork on my part, an estimate based on shaky presentiments—I noticed a hut in one of these valleys. There was no sign that anyone was living here. The windows were locked but the door was open, the chimney was not blocked, the gate broken into. When I came closer I realized that it wasn't that the door was open, there simply was no door. Later I saw the bolts still stood on the doorframe, but the door was not behind the house or in front of it. I looked up the slope I'd come down. How could that man carry the door up that way? Only on his head, like I had carried my hat. What if it had been a woman? I sat on the threshold to muse on this. I pictured the woman, strong, pretty, with a stinging sense of humor. I imagined how she strained, licked her lips, lifted an oak door to her head, and departed, her wide skirt bouncing with every step, exposing her strong calves and fat thighs. Then I wondered: what if someone were watching me from the darkness while I sit here? Sudden movements stir suspicion, so do slow ones, but in this situation one can't experiment. I turned with moderate speed, which would not have given anyone reason to misunderstand me, but which also did not eliminate my chance of presenting myself with dignity. All of this was unnecessary: no one was in the hut, no glimmer of bloodthirsty eyes, no growling of cramped animals, no stench of rotten corpses. A little later, when I grew accustomed to the dark, I noticed the door. It was standing in the corner, its upper edge leaning against the wall, it even had its handle. I lifted it, or rather, I tried to lift it, and then the thought of the strong woman evaporated. I knocked it over, and through the cloud of dust that was raised, I dragged it to the doorway. Here I stopped, wiped the sweat and grime from my face, and saw that night was falling outside. This renewed my strength. I strained, turned the door upright, and fit it into the doorway. I could not, and never would be able to, get it onto the bolts, but it was fine as it was. The light couldn't get in, and the dark couldn't get out. In a word, I had my home.

■ □ ■ □ ■

BUTTONS

SUDDENLY, ONE DAY, ALL MY BUTTONS WERE LOOSE. THEY hung on slender threads and swung in the gusts of the autumn wind. I went to a tailor. "There is nothing we can do about this," said the tailor and sorrowfully shook his head. "Why not?" I asked, but the tailor was not prepared for further conversation. I left the shop and carefully closed the door, trying not to catch any of the buttons dragging behind me in the door. Through the shop window I saw the tailor bend over, spit on the tips of his fingers, and tap the bottom of a large black iron. His daughter stepped out of the shop. I didn't know it was his daughter, but then she said, "Please try to understand my father. He is old, frail, his stitches are no longer even, and he protects himself with pride. He may seem to be turning down jobs beneath his station, but in fact he turns down everything. I can sew your buttons on for you." I agreed. She took me on a detour to back stairs that led up to their living room. By then, moreover, it was getting dark, though this was simply because of thick clouds and nothing else. The girl asked me to step behind the screen and give her my clothes: all the ones that had buttons. I gave her my coat, my suit jacket, my trousers, my shirt. I hesitated with the drawers; all sorts of things went through my mind, like were they clean enough, or would one discomfort (mine) provoke another (the girl's). It was simpler, however, to do up a button than to tie a drawstring, so I added my drawers to the other items of clothing and handed them out with my bare arm to the girl who was waiting on the other side of the screen. Then I sat down. The screen was all one color, nearly black. The folds in the screen were covered with cloth, so that the demarcated corner was completely dark, nearly black—all but one point, to the left, through which light shone, golden. I leaned over and peered through it. The tailor's daughter was engrossed in sewing on the buttons, biting the thread with her teeth, testing the button with her fingers. I coughed. "Are you cold?" asked the girl. "Oh, no," I answered. Then I saw that my fingers and toes were turning blue. "It won't be long," announced the girl. And, indeed, I soon received my drawers, then the shirt, then the trousers, then the suit jacket, and finally the coat. But before she handed me the coat, as soon as I had gotten the jacket and put it on, I stepped out from behind the screen and halted in the middle of the room. The tailor's daughter's long, curved neck was covered with a pale fuzz. She bit through the last thread and gave me my coat. "Do you want me to iron it for you?" she asked. I was startled. I had never before pictured an iron on my coat. I thanked her politely and offered to pay the bill. The girl refused; gently but firmly she refused. "But your father," I said and pointed to the floor, assuming, of course, that the shop was under my feet. The girl was implacable. "Well, you cannot refuse a box of chocolates and a bouquet of roses," I said. "I can't," said the tailor's daughter.

My friends were amazed. "Who sewed up your buttons?" they exclaimed. Only then did I notice the plight of their buttons. Pitiful, simply pitiful. I have not seen such a sorry sight in ages. Everything dangled, swung, held on by knots, survived with patches. Many of the buttons were chipped, mutilated, most were not where they were meant to be, and the metal ones groaned under the weight of rust and filth. I preferred to say nothing; actually, I told them that I had done it, for nothing in the world would I permit someone else to see the fuzz on her neck thinning and giving way to the tender skin on her back. My friends, of course, were incredulous. They asked me to show them my hands, to convince them with my pricked and swollen fingertips. In vain I spoke of thimbles. Nothing convinced them.

I went to a candy store and asked for a box of chocolates. "What sort of chocolates?" asked the salesgirl. I walked out.

At home I thought it over carefully. The salesgirl was right. It wasn't her fault if I was careless. I did not open the door for the friend who was knocking just then. Instead I called to him that I wasn't feeling well. "What's wrong?" asked my friend through the door. "I am thinking," I answered. "Do you want me to bring you some water?" asked my friend. He offered me aspirin, "tiger ointment," too, suggested he could massage my neck, insisted that he would be glad to walk on my back. "No," I said, standing by the desk, "I'll stay in bed."

I went to a second candy store and asked for a box of chocolates. "What sort of chocolates would you like?" asked the salesgirl. "Liquid centers," I said. "Good choice," said the salesgirl. She went to the corner, and from the highest shelf she brought down a box of chocolates wrapped in white paper. "If you wish," she said, "we can rewrap it in fancy paper." I didn't want her to. "These are the best chocolates with liquid centers," said the clerk, "and you were lucky to get them today, because by tomorrow they'll be gone." She spun round and began speaking in another direction, so I had to strain to hear her words. "There are only twelve left," she said, presumably referring to boxes of chocolates, "and yesterday there were twenty-three." She turned back to face me, and said in a clear voice, "It would be simple to figure the number of boxes sold per day, and the factor of probability of future sales on the basis of the demand when we run out of stock." I did not know how to reply; she, in fact, hadn't asked me anything. We stood there for a few more minutes, and then I paid, and, with the box of chocolates under my arm, I strode out into the street.

The box of chocolates was on the desk in my study when my mother knocked at the door. "Mother," I said when I opened the door, "what are you doing here?" "I don't want to talk about it," said my mother. Then she pointed to the box wrapped in white paper, which lay on the desk in my study. "What have you got there?" she asked. I peered toward the study as if I were in my apartment for the first time. "Oh, that," I said, feeling my voice was betraying me. "Those are copies of my old letters." Mother moved toward the door of my study. "Why did you wrap them all up like that?" she asked. "To preserve them," I said, "from dust, moisture, bookworms, and from myself. You know how I can be." "I know," said my mother. An expression of concern crossed her face. "Don't tell me your attacks are more frequent now," she said. "They aren't," I answered, "don't worry," and patted her on the outstretched hand that was not touching my cheek. "Oh, God," sighed my mother, "I was *so* worried."

I went into a flower shop and said I wanted to buy some tulips. "But sir," said the salesperson, "there are no tulips now. I'm terribly sorry, but it's not their season yet." "Fine," I said, "then give me a bouquet of roses."

With my box of chocolates under my left arm and the bouquet of roses in my left hand, I tapped, with my right index finger, on the tailor's door. His daughter opened. "Don't be angry," she said, when I gave her the roses and chocolates, "if I am not overjoyed by your gifts, though they do warm my heart, because at this moment my father is very ill." By then we were already inside the shop, and I immediately put my hand on the doorknob, ready to leave. "No," said the girl, "don't go!" She stretched out her hand to prevent me, and really did touch my elbow, but dropped the box of chocolates. I lifted the chocolates, noting, of course, the bits of dust and strands of thread sticking to the white paper wrapping. I sat near the iron. The tailor's daughter sat on a stool. She didn't let go of the smudged box of chocolates and the bouquet of roses. In the silence that surrounded both of us I could hear the gentle squeaking of the bed in the room above us. The girl noticed my gaze toward the ceiling, and said, "That is my father. He is bedridden, it is very trying for him. I take him warm milk in the morning, soup at noon, in the evening I fry him up liver, but he hardly takes a mouthful. I'm frightened." I knelt, took the box of chocolates and roses from her hands, placed them on the table, and buried my head in her skirt. I have always loved it when they stroke my hair. When I raised my head a little later, I saw the girl was asleep. Who knows how many nights she had sat by her father's side, and now exhaustion had overcome her. I slipped my hand under her skirt and touched the upper edge of her stocking, felt the quality of her slip, the fasteners on her garter belt. She wore no underpants. Then the girl stretched and said, "I have to go up and check on him. Thanks for the gifts." I asked her, "Does that mean that it is time for me to go? Or do you want me to wait?" "You know what my father is like," the girl said. Then we heard dull thuds above our heads. "Oh well," said the girl, "he's summoning me. He has woken up and he wants to . . . " "Will I see you again?" I asked. I was still kneeling, though she now stood. "Come tomorrow," she said, and ran up the stairs. These inside stairs couldn't have led up to the same place the outside ones did. I stood up with some effort, brushing the dust from my knees and checking my buttons. There seemed to be voices coming from above, but in the growing dark it was easy to be fooled.

A friend of mine came to visit and announced that he had come to speak in the name of all the rest. "How many of you are there?" I asked him. My friend ignored the question and said, "I don't want this to sound like a threat or extortion, but the sorry state of our buttons has forced us to take this step. Under other conditions, or in some novel, ours would be an act of despair. We, however, are relying on your understanding, your generosity, on your bonds to us all. Your heart has opened to us so many times, it couldn't possibly harden now." He fell silent. I coughed. He coughed. I waited. He spoke again: "You must tell us who fixed your buttons. A great deal more than the simple benefit to us as individual beings is at stake . . . the serenity of the universe, if you will." "What if I refuse?" I asked. "We will have to abandon you," my friend said. "All of you?" I asked. "All of us," he confirmed. "But how many of you are there?"

The next day I went back to the tailor. My buttons were still in place, which gave me a feeling of self-confidence. I knocked, and the door was opened by my mother. "Mother," I exclaimed, "what are you doing here?" "I do not want to talk about it," said my mother, and retreated back into the shop. Then I caught sight of the tailor. He was licking his fingers, tapping the bottom of the black iron, then lowering it onto a moist cloth patch. A little cloud of steam rose from the patch. The tailor's daughter sat by the window and skillfully hemmed a piece of cloth. I figured it might be somebody's pocket, but first I wanted to know what was going on. "What is going on here?" I asked. The tailor turned and looked at me. He held the iron aloft, as if afraid that its very proximity might set something on fire, cause a conflagration. "Do not bother the man," said my mother. The tailor's daughter started at the sound of her voice, the needle jabbed through the cloth, and shortly we could see a drop of blood on her palm. "Quick," I said, "hand me alcohol and gauze." Then the tailor said, "If you keep this up, I will clobber you with this iron." At that moment I realized the importance and value of the friends I no longer had. The iron wobbled in the tailor's hand. Where was the needle? My mother spoke again, her voice a squawk, "You are needlessly pestering all of us." Fine, I thought, and turned, but I didn't know where to go. The darkness was as dense outside as it was inside; light only bounced off a star, or the eye of a needle, from time to time. My mother and the tailor breathed hoarsely, alternating, while his daughter could be heard sobbing briefly, interspersed by long pauses. I wondered whether in the pauses between the sobs she was sleeping and whatever had become of her underpants. I never saw them. Were they drying, perhaps, on a clothesline in the backyard? Then my mother spoke again. "Has he gone?" she asked. "Yes," said the tailor. "I'll turn on the light," said the girl. And when the light was finally turned on, I was nowhere to be seen.

▪ ▫ ▪ ▫ ▪

THE POPE

WHEN MENDOZA CROSSES HIMSELF IN FRONT OF THE TELEVI-sion camera on his way off the soccer field, the Pope sits bolt upright, excited. He looks around, but the cardinals are sleeping peacefully in their easy chairs. Mendoza vanishes from the screen. For a moment the Pope again feels the burden of solitude, but then the game continues, and he succumbs to the inarticulate passions of soccer.

. . .

The Pope loves to talk with soldiers. They tell him about faraway places he has never been. "I would love to be a soldier," thinks the Pope as he stops before troops standing in rows. The soldiers have arrived from far away. They are grimy, caked with sweat and blood. Some can hardly stand, some doze, leaning on their lances. "Soldier," the Pope addresses a lanky soldier and notices the youthful hairs on his upper lip, "can you tell me what Jerusalem looks like?" The soldier tries to puff out his chest, and the Pope notices how his muscles are trembling from the strain and exhaustion. "When I got there," the soldier says, "all I saw was ashes."

. . .

In strolling along long corridors, the Pope first notices the symmetry of repetition. When he lifts his head, he sees arabesques, the meaning of which he cannot fathom. "Why should everything have meaning?" wonders the Pope in a whisper, then quickly bites his tongue and darts glances in all directions. These days even the walls have ears.

. . .

The Pope wakes early. The window is open, the air fresh, the sky blue, etc. The Pope gets up, tripping on his long nightshirt, and notices a bird on the windowsill. The Pope goes back to the night table, but nothing is left of last night's sandwich. "Birdie," says the Pope to the bird, "will you wait while I send someone for a little bread?" The bird does not reply. "Or would you prefer grains—wheat or millet?" The bird keeps quiet. The Pope lifts the receiver and calls the central warehouse. A sleepy voice says, "Hello?" "Is there any millet in the warehouse?" asks the Pope. "Who's asking?" repeats the voice. "Forget it," says the Pope and puts the receiver back down.

. . .

For ages he didn't know there were mirrors. Then one day he was taken to a room where the countless smooth surfaces bounced back reflections of his face. For a moment the Pope could imagine a world full of popes, and he clucked his tongue in delight. Then he called in a handyman and asked him to take all the mirrors down. He kept only one, in the attic, which no one knew of.

. . .

If there is one thing he hates, it is mornings. Every time he wakes up, it seems, he finds his nightshirt has twisted all the way up to his chin. "I would rather sleep in pajamas," says the Pope, and angrily stamps his foot. The cardinals exchange glances. "And I've had it with this nightcap," howls the Pope and flings the cap from his head. The cap drops onto lined silken slippers, a gift from the Turkish ambassador. "Our regulations do not permit it," a cardinal finally dares to speak. Regulations, thinks the Pope, damnation. I should have stayed an ordinary village priest.

. . .

The Pope writes poems. A journalist asks him, "In your case, might one speak, indeed, of divine inspiration?" The Pope has read *Faust,* and he knows where this question is leading. So he does not respond. The cardinal who is the Pope's press attaché speaks up: "Any other questions?" The Pope feels beads of sweat on his forehead like the touch of someone's icy hand.

. . .

Morning meetings, official noon luncheons, afternoon preparations for the next day—only in the evening (before and after Vespers) does the Pope have a bit of time to himself. He sits by a window and gazes into the sky. Of all that he sees there he likes the clouds best. Each cloud is shaped differently. Some look like familiar things, others like things soon to be invented, yet others suggest distant worlds, and some dissolve as the Pope watches. Footsteps heard from the depths of the palace belong to a young monk who brings the Pope his chamber pot. The Pope would gladly speak with the young man, but the monk cut off his own tongue so that he could pledge all his thoughts to God. What nonsense, thinks the Pope. The monk sets the pot behind the door, covers it with a richly embroidered cloth, bows, and leaves.

. . .

The Pope is alone. Nothing interests him. He has leafed through the Holy Gospels but could not find a single passage he did not already know by heart. He could call someone on the phone, but whom? He used to entertain himself by dialing random numbers on the phone, and then he'd giggle into his sleeve when some irate (male or female) voice barked: "Hello! Hello? Who's there?" But the Pope feels that he has outgrown such petty diversions. Now he'd rather imagine a world in which there are at least two Popes. He'd have someone else to play dominoes or chess with. Imagine if there were three! Cards! The Pope goes over to the desk, flicks on his computer, and enters the question: "When will the next ecumenical council be held?" The computer replies: "The year 2012." The Pope types: "But I won't be alive by then." "You won't," replies the computer, "but the Pope will."

. . .

Is this my true face? muses the Pope, leaning over the sink. It is difficult to discern the precise state of affairs on the rippled water surface, but the Pope does think that he has bushy eyebrows, long lashes, and blue eyes. The Pope scoops up water and splashes his face. When the water surface is still again, when he can see himself in it, he is certain his eyes are black.

. . .

The Pope strolls around the yard. The yard is surrounded by a high wall. Every time he reaches the wall the Pope listens. He can hear nothing. No sound comes from beyond the wall. Perhaps there is nothing out there, thinks the Pope. Maybe I am alone in the world. Apples and pears drop behind his back; ripe fruit falls onto the mowed lawn. "Hey," shouts the Pope, "is anyone there?" Silence, silence, nothing but silence.

. . .

In the middle of a sermon, once, at a moment of tranquil solemnity, as the Pope was raising an index finger to make his closing sentence emphatic, one of the faithful rose and in a resounding voice asked, "How can the Pope know the truth about family life? Who has a wife and children? Him or us?" Since the question was not addressed directly to the Pope, the Pope—like everyone else—looked around, but no one tried to respond. Maybe I should suggest an answer, thought the Pope, but then he noticed his uplifted index finger. Never had he seen his finger so illuminated! This is a divine sign, thought the Pope. With unconcealed anticipation, he twisted his neck to peer up into the dome. But it was dark up there, so very dark up there, and the Pope was afraid of the dark. He brought his index finger to his face, cautiously, as if brandishing a torch, and then he fainted.

. . .

The Pope is certain that life has no beginning and no end. It simply changes features: today we are this, tomorrow that. The Pope, of course, cannot explain how or why the number of people keeps growing. Has the quantity of lives remained the same, finding outlet in a larger number of human beings? Does this mean that people are becoming more numerous thanks to the extinction of certain animal species? Maybe I was once a dodo, muses the Pope. He pictures himself on one of the Indian Ocean islands, and sees the Spanish or the Dutch conquistadors as they come to him with a grin and an unsheathed sword. Do not approach me, he warns them, I am the Pope! But the Spaniard is quick, experienced; he knows, like the Dutchman, that the dodo is a stupid and helpless bird, endlessly naive and gullible. Come, dodo, come, come, sing the conquerors. And then: the flash of the sword, the smell of blood, warm soup, a roasted drumstick, discarded innards thrown behind the palisades, which even dogs won't sniff.

. . .

The Pope kneels and talks with a six-year-old boy. They are in an orphanage at Saint Catherine's, or Saint Isabella's, or Saint Dominique's, or Saint Genevieve's. So many immaculate women, thinks the Pope, in this, the worst of all worlds: nothing short of incredible! He makes a final stab at urging the little boy to talk, but the boy is intractable. The Pope knows what comes next: either the boy will start to cry or stick out his tongue. His sweet, smooth, pink little tongue! The Pope, of course, would prefer the tongue, but one never can be sure with these rascals. The Pope gets up, resting in passing on the boy's shoulder (so small, so fragile), and takes the opportunity to tweak the child stealthily by his bright red ear. The Pope learned this trick in his younger years on the streets of V. and B., before they delivered him to the seminary. And so when he steps back and hears the child's howl (reminding him poignantly of the Inquisition), the Pope turns and shrugs helplessly, while one of the robust nuns tries to soothe the boy by saying, "Don't cry, son, the Pope will visit us again."

. . .

Am I a good man? wonders the Pope. He sits in a large, empty room in which all sounds are oddly amplified. When he moves his foot and his rheumatic knee cracks, all the saints seem to tumble from the walls. Maybe goodness is somehow related to staying still? The Pope pulls the silken cord: although he hears nothing he knows that in the depths of the Vatican a mechanism is set in motion, which, a moment later, will appear at the door in the form of the young dumb monk with the chamber pot in his hands. "This must be a mistake," says the Pope, "I summoned the cardinals, not you." The monk shrugs, smiles, and moves toward the door. "But, no matter," says the Pope, "come here." The monk comes over, and the Pope takes him by the hand. "Tell me," says the Pope, "am I a good man?" The monk's eyes fly open, he gropes for the right facial expression, and then he opens his mouth. The Pope first sees the stump of his tongue, strangely thick and lumpy, then he hears a voice that embodies all voices. Then the walls begin to crumble.

. . .

The Pope sits by a well. He feels chilly, but no one thinks to bring him a mantle. I'll catch a cold here, thinks the Pope, and it may kill me. And still no one brings him a mantle. It will rain soon, then frost, then snow. At least I have enough water, thinks the Pope, and leans his forehead on the stone well wall. "If you have no fire, use ice": so said a proverb he read long ago in a manuscript from the secret chamber of the Vatican library. Another said: "In order to return, first you must leave." One is from Iceland, the other, Polynesia. The world is so big, thinks the Pope, while the seams in the stone press into the refined skin of his forehead. If someone were to see me from some vast height, he thinks on, I would be no more than a miserable speck in the infinitude of God's garden, but who could see from such a distance? A moment later the first drop of rain falls on his neck. The Pope lifts his head to take a look at how far the clouds have come (perhaps someone has brought him an umbrella after all?), but instead of clouds he sees a huge eye on the blue dome of the sky.

. . .

The Pope is ninety-nine years old. He has long since stopped eating, sleeping, and receiving visitors. He stares unswervingly at the velvet curtain behind which, he is convinced, God resides. He does not know where he has gotten this notion, why velvet and God seem associated—perhaps the particular rough smoothness of the fabric? Who knows? The Pope would gladly dismiss this with a wave of his hand, but he cannot move it. He continues to stare at the velvet curtain, longing for even the slightest trembling of its folds. God, however, remains silent, hesitating. The Pope recalls his life's most cherished moment: when he sat at a marble sweetshop table, still a boy, and they served him a large dish of ice cream. When the curtain finally does move, the Pope is not surprised when, instead of God, he sees a smiling waitress in a short skirt with dimples in her cheeks. Or is this, perhaps, God's countenance? It no longer matters, the Pope knows. He closes his eyes, sticks out his tongue, and takes the last rites—with the drowsy aroma of vanilla.

■ □ ■ □ ■

MUTE SONG

SOMETIMES THE LEGEND COMES BEFORE THE PERSON, OTHER times after.

The latter is more straightforward: after the person has gone, has faded into oblivion, the collective imagination turns him or her into the subject of a story, true at first, but which in time, especially in the instance of the eruption of new forms of violence, edges farther and farther from the historical truth and begins to dwell, for itself alone, within the context of some irrational logic all its own. Hmmm.

The former is far more serious: after a legend is created—which has tried since the very beginning to elude every twist of history—someone appears who fits it to a T. Here one can surely doubt the collective imagination. The initiator is probably some loner, a visionary perhaps, maybe a prophet, a sly shyster—why not?—who has set in motion some incredible story, into which he himself later moves.

Be that as it may, the legend of ◬ existed before ◬ did. It is well known that the art of writing names on the inner walls of buses in the Belgrade public transit system flourished in the mid-1970s, just when omnipotent and all-seeing conductors were replaced by red ticket-punching machines. There are suggestions, however, that the sign ◬ appeared for the first time as early as the late *1960s*. This occurred in a trolley bus, at a time when the capital city was still entirely baffled by and unprepared for the incursion of counterculture. The facts are hard to substantiate. It is hard, though not impossible, to imagine that △ brought a Magic Marker, still a rare commodity in Belgrade, back from some trip of his abroad and tried it out on the grimy white interior of a city vehicle. Perhaps △ was seen by some boy who would, a decade later, raise *his* marker, certainly with a wider tip, and remember. A legend in the making: in a flash, while the body, borne through space, relaxes and submits to itself, to its mind, to its spirit, to the collective permeating everything.

According to another version, △, under a different name, was thought, during the 1960s, to be a sly freeloader, so clever that he could board the bus even with the inspectors, and still outwit them and get away scot-free. This romantic version interprets the △ phenomenon as follows: Unsnarable, despite his name, was snared only once (here there are numerous miniversions of why and how this happened). The cops took him off the bus at what was an auxiliary stop near the Federal Executive Council Building. They took him across the street, cautiously, into thick bushes. The sky was clear until then, but at that moment, from the west, dark clouds began to roil. The cops pounded him systematically, as if they were acting in some local movie, until they began to tire. △, or rather Unsnarable, was left lying on the ground when the cops, feeling the first drops of rain on their sweaty necks, ran off toward the street. Unsnarable lifted his hand and felt his jaw, lips, nose, forehead. He could see blood on the tips of his fingers and felt a wave of nausea. The storm picked up force. The raindrops swelled to the size of chicken eggs. Unsnarable knew he would never stand again: his legs were broken, his spine crushed, his belly smeared all over the grass and leaves. He would become earth and stay earth. At that moment the wind blew an empty sheet of paper toward him, and Unsnarable, with his last ounce of strength, traced the sign △ in blood on the paper. The wind then shrieked like a creature, like a beast, and lifted the piece of paper high into the sky. This note, this holy inscription, thereby submitted to no one and everyone, is believed to be held somewhere for safekeeping, even today, but where?

Whatever the case, people spoke of ◬, they'd heard of ◬. The Graffiti-writers' Association had triangle-shaped membership cards, the same shaped rubber stamp, a similar insignia on their envelopes. Their members could be recognized by a small ◬ tattooed above the left eyebrow. Aside from that, what set them apart from your garden-variety graffiti artists, who frantically scribbled their names hundreds of times, was the fact that they were forbidden (under the threat of who knows what punishment) to write in buses at all, unless they really had something to say or in cases of extreme necessity, especially the holy sign. Therefore, every ◬ seen in public was a lie, a revolting lie, a counterfeit. But the plebes inevitably craved whatever the nobility considered noblesse oblige, and their single victory could be to deglorify it, to bring it down to earth, to belittle it. ◬ was a demystification of ◬.

Who had actually seen such membership cards? Who handled the rubber stamp? Who had ever received in the mail an envelope bearing such an insignia? No one. These are all nothing but conjecture: dough made with rotten yeast (if there is such a thing); all of this is what, when farthest from the truth, seems closest to it.

One more interpretation should be mentioned, an explanation that is thought to come from the back rooms of the first feminist gathering in Belgrade, held at the Student Cultural Center. Since the local feminist movement has its roots in Zagreb, one can readily believe that this interpretation originated in some Zagreb Upper Town café, probably during a cozy tête-à-tête between two women, quiet at first glance, soft-spoken, with pauses, with broad grins, while lightly fingering the lapels on one another's corduroy jackets and the sleeves of their roomy, comfortable blouses. The wine, white, in front of them swayed in the glasses. Both of them looked like the female protagonist in *Last Tango in Paris*. Several months later, in Belgrade, it was all set. Some even referred to the signing of a secret document; others were more restrained: according to them, an oral agreement had been reached, which had been adopted at the last meeting—each participant would respond with a predetermined signal when given a sign by a certain person. This was what it came down to: △ did, in fact, exist—as a symbol, of course—but its true origin was far from what the male chauvinist clique had claimed in its typically exploitative way. △ did not begin as a bloody symbol scratched on some nebulous scrap of paper; its beginning was indeed in blood, but it first surfaced as ▽. Where? The Vasa Stajić Reformatory in Zemun. When? The late 1950s. In one of the corner dorm rooms the JDs—look-alikes, heads shaved —were busy at their favorite Saturday ritual: taking turns fucking Fat Mara (the symbol of downtrodden, postwar woman?), who only giggled and wiggled her wobbly thighs all the more. Then Keža the Lump suddenly thought of a girl who had been brought to the reformatory a week before, who hadn't spoken a word to anyone. He thought of her just when he was standing, his pants dropped, between Mara's legs, staring at his limp penis. The rest of them egged him on with chosen words, but to no avail. Mita the Hippo suggested tickling his balls. Pera the Fart offered his own sincere hand. Keža the Lump, however, thought of Liberty (a cleverly chosen name, yet another symbol), and his prick popped up taller than it had ever had been. The erection was so big that they all stopped talking. It soared up and pointed in such an obvious direction that they turned to see what was there. At the back of the dorm room, by the window, her forehead on the pane, stood Liberty. A ray of light lit her face. Silence. Bring her here, Keža the Lump finally spoke, and after that everything happened fast, very fast. Mita the Hippo and Smaja brought her over. She didn't even resist, though she may well have figured, though she probably knew exactly what to expect. Pera the Fart took off the sheet; Keža the Lump came over and put Liberty (oh, she was so light, how light she was!) on the table. Her skirt was made of some soft fabric, and when he lifted it up he saw clean, white underwear. Someone unbuttoned her blouse; one button ripped off and dropped on the floor. "Forget it," said Keža the Lump when Dule leaned over. Her breasts were pretty small and firm, and no one touched them. He parted her legs. "I want you to watch," said Keža the Lump. Mita the Hippo squeezed her neck so she couldn't turn her head away. Keža's prick had grown so huge by then that she went all stiff and lifted her buttocks a little off the table when he pushed his way in. "Watch," moaned Keža the Lump, "watch."

"I am watching," said Liberty, and Fat Mara began to giggle.

When Keža the Lump pulled it out, they all saw the blood. When he left her, at the end, Liberty got down off the table and stood there, her legs still apart. Her knees were wobbly, she was thirsty, her stomach hurt. She touched the place between her legs, and though her palm was wet, she felt a soothing coolness. She took a few trembling steps, and when she looked down at that same (left) palm, she saw on it, in the gloom, the sign of ▽ etched in blood, the insignia of her insides, the stamp of her vagina. The next day, no, it was Monday, someone came for her, took her away. Keža the Lump was run over by a bus. Mita the Hippo was stabbed by Zemun thugs from the quay. Pera the Fart died of pneumonia. Smaja, after many years, found he had colon cancer. Fat Mara died in gynecological stirrups. Only Dule was spared, but he had poor hearing and sight.

So ends this rambling tale. Male consumer society, the feminists claimed, had taken the women's model and adjusted it to their needs. The triangle, a symbol of femininity, the tip turned down toward Mother Earth, the fertility symbol, was rotated so that the tip pointed up, skyward, ensconced as a symbol of rigidity, a phallic symbol that—with its broad base resting on Earth—drains everything from it and channels it upward to the Sovereign of the Skies. They changed the dot, a man surrounded by a triangle of women, to a dot, a woman hedged by a male triangle. The △ that appeared in the Belgrade vehicles of public transport was a subverted expression of women's power. Under every △ there was a hidden ▽; it's just that no one could see it.

Not nearly enough, none of this is enough.

The only things left, after all else, are words.

How about a song?

When Kate Davis, a student at the University of California, finally learned that she had received a Fulbright fellowship, which would allow her to spend at least a year in Yugoslavia, she went back to her room, sat at her desk, and took out a sheet of stationery. Whom could she write to, anyway? She turned to the window, noticing as she moved the movement of her features in the mirror. She couldn't see much. It was late spring, early summer, and the sky—so she could see sky—the sky was taut, blue, cloudless. The title of her imaginary thesis appeared to her clear as day, "Vocal Singing Styles of Croatia," a work that would not be so long as it would be exhaustive, detailed, and indisp-p-p-pensable . . . Why was she stuttering? She got up, this time went right over to the mirror. The reflection of her hand glimmered on the smooth surface of the table lamp. She had long, smooth hair, which she loved to touch in the pitch dark before she fell asleep at night. She tried to remember some words she'd learned at her intermittent Serbo-Croatian lessons. She couldn't recall a single one. She stared at herself in the mirror and felt a perfect void in her head. She knew that there must be some meaning to that silence, but at the same time she knew that she'd only find it if she wasn't looking. She stepped back, took a bag with her notebooks and writing utensils that she had tossed onto the bed a moment before, touched her face, her blouse, her face again, and left for the library, where she spent the next weeks in exhaustive preparation for her departure.

First she skimmed a dusty mound of journals: *Journal of the Society for Ethnomusicology, Journal of the International Folk Music Council, Journal of Popular Culture.* She leafed through, until her eyes were bleary with the unfamiliar words and strange letters, yearly *Folklore* and *Narodna umjetnost* volumes, then *Zbornik za narodni život i običaje.* She wrote a letter to the Institute for Research in Folklore, the Institute for Philology and Folklore Studies in Zagreb (they told her that she might be going to Zagreb). She got to know a girl who was also using the old journals, looking for historical data on Montenegro. The girl told her that Yugoslavia was a beautiful country with ugly cities and nice people, and she warned her of their "essential simplicity." So, by the time she'd gotten a courteous answer from Zagreb, she had immersed herself in the works of earlier students, to which Charles J. Brown, acting department chair, had drawn her attention. By the fall, therefore, when there were just a few days left before her departure, she picked up the last master's thesis, "An Ethnographic Study of Three Villages of the Lika Region of Yugoslavia," and she sat at a desk in the library where she had, with ballpoint pen, in one out-of-the-way corner, written her initials: K. D. She read the introduction, which stood apart from the other things she'd read because of the scholarliness of its approach, then a section on agriculture, on customs, on costumes, on the folk calendar . . . She looked back at the title page, and only then did she notice that there was no author's name there. She turned to the last page in the hope that she'd find it there, then back to the first, and then—raising her eyebrows and shrugging, unaware that her features were reflected in a distant windowpane—she went on reading. She came to the section on the music of that region, on the songs and dances, and here, in the part that carried the heading "Mute

Kolo," she came across the footnote she had been waiting for her whole life, the end of everything and the beginning of everything:

> 49) The mute kolo dance appears in other parts of Yugoslavia as well, but the author will dwell here on the Lika variants alone. Perhaps it would be wise to note that the author once came across the term "mute song" as well, but while one can speak of the mute kolo with certainty—the author was present on several occasions when such dances were performed, and there is quite a wealth of literature on the mute kolo (see appended bibliography)—we have been able to find almost nothing on the "mute song." The author came across the term itself during a conversation with an elderly man while traveling through the northern portion of Lika, but there is no way of telling whether it is limited only to the Lika region. One might be predisposed to think otherwise. The elderly man claimed that he knew a "mute song"; when he was urged to perform it, he refused to do so, saying that, after all, it was "mute." (Included is a transcription of a conversation which the author recorded on tape; most of the recorded interview is not, however, fully comprehensible.) The author: "How can someone sing silence?" The old man: "You don't sing the silence . . . it sings you. You are merely the vessel." Author: "When would you sing a 'mute song'?" Old man: "When I feel that someone else knows it." Author: "Pardon?" Old man: "When I feel that someone else or several others know it so we can sing it together." Author: "Do you mean you are silent together?" Old man: "We're singing, you're silent." Author: "Are you from Lika?" Old man (laughing): "No one knows where he's from." Author: "But you were born here?" Old man: "Here . . . there . . . everywhere . . . "

> Author: "How old are you?" Old man (laughing): "Plenty . . . plenty to . . . [garbled section] . . . who knows . . . " After this, the old man refused to speak any further. None of the people to whom the author later spoke about the "mute song" could tell him anything. Quite by chance, in a used bookstore in Belgrade, the author came across a slender volume, *A Description of Our Folk Songs and Dances,* by one V. Pecić (published by Napredak, Belgrade, 1924), which mentions the "mute song" twice: the first time as the name of the song that accompanies the mute kolo, and the second time in an extremely unclear context. While the first mention is obviously a terminological blunder, the second is probably a typographical error. Although the very idea of a "mute song" is undoubtedly an appealing one, we must, it seems, conclude that it does not, in fact, exist. In all the literature available to us on the musical traditions of other countries, we have never come across mention of a similar notion.

This is it, she said to herself, as if she were convincing someone else. The out-of-the-way corner where the desk with her initials on it stood had become more visible, and no matter where she was in the library at any moment she could spot it. She photocopied the footnote, jotted down a few more details, organized the rest of her notes, packed up most of the things she owned, and wrote her mother's address on the package in large letters. She was leaving, finally she knew she was leaving. The night before her departure—though it wasn't quite—she was leaving for New York, where she would spend four or five days (with her friends in Brooklyn, at 15 Diamond Street), and only then take the plane for Frankfurt and beyond—she spent with Ann Margaret, certainly the closest friend she'd made while a student, in her room, in her bed. Ann Margaret was a large girl, with a broad face, straight brown hair, generous breasts, upon which (the right breast!) Kate Davis was resting her head. Ann Margaret asked her whether she was sorry to be going. "I don't know," said Kate. She ran the tips of her fingers over Ann Margaret's belly, soft and supple. "There are moments when I think," she went on, "that with this departure everything will be resolved, and then there are others, again, when I feel like it is closing everything off, though in a kind of way, I have this presentiment that a lot of things *will* be resolved there. Imagine," she almost laughed, "of all the places in the world, in Yugoslavia I'll meet my destiny . . . "

"Yeah," said Ann Margaret. But she'd stopped talking.

"What?" asked Ann Margaret.

"I don't know," said Kate, "it is as if, as if I'm frightened, as if, I don't know, I wonder whether I shouldn't have stayed. You don't master things in the world by moving but by staying still, you know?"

"I know," said Ann Margaret. The fingers of her right hand curved around the back of Kate's head.

"I know that it sounds crazy," whispered Kate, "but I have this feeling that I'll disappear completely there."

"Don't worry," said Ann Margaret, "they aren't all maniacs."

"No," replied Kate, "not that way, not disappear physically—how can I say this?—in spirit, maybe."

"Yes," said Ann Margaret. "Come here." She drew Kate's face to her and rolled onto her hip so that she was looking down at her face. First she felt her skin, then her breath. Then her tongue, sharp as a knife, parted, after feeble resistance, Kate Davis's lips. And that is how they parted.

The gloomy story she'd heard from the chance acquaintance in the library stacks turned out to be true. What she saw of the countryside, while she rode in an uncomfortable train from Germany to Zagreb, really was beautiful. She spent a week in Zagreb, long enough to ascertain that the people really were nice and that the city, despite a certain classical serenity, was not attractive. While she strolled around the streets she was plagued by a strange sense of borders, sundering, collapse, something that she only managed to pinpoint when she arrived in Belgrade (for, they told her, she would be staying in Belgrade). She figured it out when she saw that city straining to fill the Western shapes of a metropolis in an Eastern mode: with noise, chaos, and disorder. She understood what it means to be on the boundary between East and West, not to belong to anyone, to be neither one nor the other. Her first thought was: go home. The fear she had tried to show to Ann Margaret now showed itself to her. She feared the dark. She feared the deeply set eyes that would watch her, unblinking, in the bus. She was afraid of herself when she realized that pretty soon she'd stop feeling afraid. The first ten days or so she stayed with a girl whom she'd happened to meet at the American Embassy. The girl lived in a building for lower-ranking diplomatic staff, in an apartment designed to reproduce America in detail so as to prevent pollution from without. Her name was Linda, and she was extremely conservative. Kate spent that time looking for an apartment, and so it was that she stumbled upon Zemun, where she finally decided to stay, and she rented a furnished apartment on October 22nd Street.

Zemun was something different. Whether it was the river or who knows what, she didn't feel the boundary that had been hovering like a knife blade in the air. She fell in love with the Tower, at the foot of which, some six months later, she wrote a poem. Moved by an inexplicable melancholy, she sent it to the first boy she'd ever gone out with. She began to jog, and she jogged every morning, sometimes alone, sometimes with other joggers, along the Danube, by Hotel Yugoslavia across from the Federal Executive Council Building, almost all the way to the confluence of the rivers. Slowly she made her way through the labyrinth of the

Serbo-Croatian language, and she felt a growing sense of competence (which still required caution, she thought) whenever she went into the grocery store on the corner or the store across the street, which they had awkwardly dubbed a *dragstor*. It seemed to her that her eyes were opening more and more, that she was beginning to see things, notice details, learn, know. She wrote to Ann Margaret about it, but when she got a letter back, she decided not to write to her anymore. Loneliness approached her with large steps, and she braced herself to greet it. Soon, she sensed, she would have to leave herself in order to enter herself.

And so it happened that one afternoon, sunny and warm despite the late season, from her seat at the back of the bus, she noticed a small group of people on some ridiculous, artificial hill next to Hotel Yugoslavia. A sharp pain stabbed her heart. She got up and made her way to the exit. She stepped out right into a gust of wind. The stop was at the other end of the long hotel building, and she walked back, trying not to break into a run. When she had crossed the second street, she could see them more clearly. There were six of them, four men and two blond women. They were standing, scattered randomly, at first glance, on the hilltop, but Kate recognized the pattern. She passed by one of the men and didn't see anything in his eyes. One step more, two more, and she found herself in her position. Then she heard the silence. And she sang the mute song.

■ □ ■ □ ■

AFTERWORD

Words and Things: David Albahari's Prose in the Context of the Former Yugoslavia

Tomislav Longinović

Duša je koka-kola u kojoj telo pluta.
[The soul is the Coca-Cola in which the body floats.]

David Albahari, "Studio Apartment"

David Albahari (b. 1948, Peć) has been one of the leading literary artists in the former Yugoslavia since the late 1970s. His deep involvement with the craft of fiction places him in the category of "literary artists" who managed to survive in a culture dominated by the "realism" of the former socialist state. The narrator-protagonist of Albahari's "Studio Apartment," a singular bachelor who drinks *vinjak* (a painfully bad substitute for French cognac), equates the soul with Coca-Cola, which, according to urban legend, dissolves the liver, kidneys, and other internal organs. If Coca-Cola stands for the soul, the ravaged Slavic soul of the nationalists is replaced by another, even more destructive one. The Coca-Cola soul corrodes the body like acid, leaving only the semiotic traces of Albahari's mourning, a mourning for the wholeness of being that got lost in the horrors of history. This kind of literature, which explores the negative side of being, positions its writer on the other side of the national-patriotic canon, which had been enforcing its hegemonic conception of literature since World War II.

Albahari's stories vary thematically from his early preoccupation with family life in a Central European cultural milieu to his later metafictional search for the roots of a writer's identity and craft. He has published nine books of literary prose, some of which have been translated into Hebrew, Italian, Hungarian, Albanian, German, Esperanto, and Polish. This selection, representative of most trends in his literary development, draws on five principal collections of shorter prose: *Porodično vreme* (Family time, 1973), *Opis smrti* (The description of death, 1982), *Fras u šupi* (Shock in a shack, 1984), *Jednostavnost* (Simplicity, 1988), and *Pelerina* (The cloak, 1993). Besides numerous literary translations from English, Albahari has also published four novels: *Sudija Dimitrijević* (Judge Dimitrijević, 1978), *Cink* (Zinc, 1988), *Kratka knjiga* (Short book, 1993), and the recent *Snežni čovek* (Snow man, 1995).

If one were to construct a literary genealogy for Albahari, his immediate ancestor would be Danilo Kiš, the first post–World War II prose writer in Yugoslavia to break decisively with the predominant national-patriotic orientation in letters. Kiš forced a significant opening in the domestic literary scene after successfully confronting the literary establishment, which had been provoked by the publication of his *Grobnica za Borisa Davidoviča* (The tomb for Boris Davidovich) in 1976. Kiš was accused of plagiarizing many domestic and foreign writers and historians, including Jorge Luis Borges. Since the Borgesian "invitation to falsify" greatly reminded Kiš of Stalinist historiographical practices, he devoted his *Tomb* to the victims of Soviet revolutionary terror of the 1930s. The book focuses its uncanny gaze on the legacy of personality cults and their totalitarian logic. The neo-Baroque tone of *The Tomb* derives from its documentary voice, which explores an alternative truth by dissecting official historiography and its claims. It indirectly challenges all those whose roots were tied to the communist movement. The awful conclusion of the "pamphlet-novel," as Kiš called *The Tomb,* identifies the continuing terror experienced by ideological/racial others as a certain consequence of totalitarianism. The heroic image of the communist is supplemented by the criminal one, while writing is treated as an essential tool for resisting the official vision of the party.

The strong cult of realism in Yugoslavia was rooted in the experience of the Second World War and in the emergent socialist literature that focused on the heroic and righteous war for liberation led by Tito and his communist partisans. The themes of sacrifice and struggle, which dominated the testimonial and literary works of former partisan warriors, were supposed to serve as a cultural backdrop for socialist Yugoslavia. In the 1940s and 1950s, the official "Yugoslavism" of the communists was expressed in this hybrid form of socialist realism, which peaked with the works of such writers as Dobrica Ćosić (Serbia), Mihajlo Lalić (Montenegro), and Branko Ćopić (Bosnia).

The career of Dobrica Ćosić is a perfect metaphor for the metamorphoses that Yugoslav literature and culture went through from 1945 to 1991. Son of a Serbian peasant, Ćosić rose through the ranks in the Second World War to become one of the leading writers of "national-liberation prose" in the 1950s. The awakening to Tito's soft totalitarianism in the late 1960s pushed Ćosić into political dissidence and a fight for "democracy" he later equated with nationalism. During the latest War of Yugoslav Succession (1991–95), Ćosić served as president of the Serbian-Montenegrin "third Yugoslavia" during an undeclared war on the territories west of the river Drina. This validated Ćosić as the true "father of the Serbian nation," which began to commit its first atrocities in Croatia and Bosnia. It was this kind of heroic and apologetic intellectual tradition that Danilo Kiš confronted head on during the tumultuous literary scandals of the 1970s.

For most of the writers of Albahari's generation, the burden of "reality" enforced by this ideological socialist-realist hybrid was unbearable because of the formulaic and often repetitious nature of its narratives. The tediousness and predictability of such prose may have been vital, however, in healing the damages of World War II, since writing was one of the rare channels for the work of mourning. "Brotherhood and Unity," the slogan of official communist doctrine, based on a deliberate forgetting of the fratricidal past, slowly became a cliché for a generation born after the war. Albahari's story about a rebellion in the Stuln Nazi camp is a great example of a direct challenge to the partisan stereotypes: Father, the main protagonist of the story, is an entirely unheroic man whose life is determined by external, contingent, historical forces.

Although both Kiš and Albahari write in the eastern variant of Serbo-Croatian, there is little in their prose that connects them to a particularly "Serbian" tradition, since the national(ist) literary canon had been obsessed with the overt treatment of historical topics tied to the Serbs and their tortured sense of national identity. Neither writer takes the Serbian national problem as the main focus of his writing, although both are shaped by the cultural climate in and around the capital city of Belgrade. Albahari's and Kiš's common Jewish heritage plays a significant role in the formation of their poetics, forcing them to always question a "reality" constructed by what Kiš had once called "the logic of the compact majority." Jewishness is constructed as a metaphor of otherness, not of essential victimhood, which was reserved for the local Serbs and their Kosovo mythology.

The period of bold literary experimentation that lasted roughly from the mid-1970s through the late 1980s came to an end with a strong resurgence of national(ist) thematics in Serbia. Kiš's premature death in 1989 was an ominous sign of the disappearance of the kind of culture that once used to flourish in Yugoslav urban centers, before ethnic intolerance and the resulting war began to force cosmopolitan ideals into the background. The heterogeneous assemblage of writers who began to write in Belgrade after Kiš's victory over the "literary nationalists" came to be known, controversially, as adherents of "young Serbian prose."

David Albahari is the most significant writer of the new generation that followed in Kiš's footsteps. His work as a writer, translator, and editor of *Književna reč* (Literary Word) continues to exert significant influence on the course of literary history both in Serbia and in the other Yugoslav successor states. He became the central figure behind the "young Serbian prose," which had often been criticized by the literary establishment for its negativism, self-absorption, and lack of interest in conventional literary genres and practices. Indeed, many of the characteristics of this new sensibility, which was characteristic of the Yugoslav "apocalypse culture" in the 1980s, had its roots in a specific Central European approach to writing manifest in the works of Franz Kafka.

If it is true that most of the great Russian writers of the latter part of the nineteenth century came out of Gogol's overcoat, then one could say with certainty that most of the great Central European writers of the twentieth century came out of Kafka's kaftan. In addition to the most popular émigré writer from the "other" Europe, Milan Kundera, other writers, including Kiš, Kazimierz Brandys, and György Konrád, have been concerned with the legacy of totalitarianism as regards the destiny of individuals and their communities. Some of the characteristics shared by Central European writers of the post-Kafkaesque tradition are anti-utopianism, a pronounced sense of irony, a condensed narrative style, and an acute awareness of the power of language to simultaneously create and destroy the traditional literary categories of character, plot, setting, and point of view.

The concern with language itself is especially prominent with another strain of writers who continue to experiment within this tradition. It is symptomatic that an entire generation of Croatian and Serbian writers was labeled as "Borgesian" by the critical establishment in the late 1960s and early 1970s. These writers read Borges immediately after he swept France in the early 1960s, where he was known as the creator of parallel worlds reflected in magical mirrors. But the Central Europeans read Borges differently, as a "linguistic realist" who was describing the effects of totalitarian mind control. If language can act as reality's other, the worlds of "propaganda" and "life" do indeed exist as two parallel universes. Since Borges was describing their reality, these writers felt obliged to use language in similar ways, exposing the effects official "reality" produced through "propaganda."

If language produces its own reality in literature, then the agency of the "writer" can be used to challenge the unquestioned word-thing bond of those who produce political reality. This rebellion in language takes place through the deliberate creation of "as-if" worlds, worlds that are aware of their own artifice and uncertainty. Albahari belongs to a group of writers (which also includes Austrians Peter Handke and Thomas Bernhard, Hungarians Péter Esterházy and Lajos Grendel, among many others in Central Europe) who cling almost narcissistically to the negative side of dominant "reality." One may also add that Albahari's poetics were significantly informed by reading and translating American metafictionalists, especially Robert Coover and Thomas Pynchon. His prose shows an awareness that the avant-garde "scream without end" is no longer possible under the conditions that postmodernity imposes on writing. Most of Albahari's prose zeroes in on the process of writing itself, never allowing the story to coalesce around a definite horizon of narration.

The first part of this selection recounts the life of a Jewish family in Yugoslavia. Ruben Rubenović, a former textiles salesman, emerges as a name around which family stories circulate, stories marked by the generic presence of the unnamed Father, Mother, and Sister. Ruben Rubenović is accompanied by Father, a survivor who earns his living as gynecologist while grappling with time and its irreversible effects on life. The future is never anticipated while the past emerges through memories that torment the protagonists. Language has been petrified by the evils of history, which writing tries to undo by directing the gaze at the parodic nature of "our very being." Essentialism of any sort provokes ironic smirks, followed immediately by compassion for the naive.

The stories of the family cycle carry the seed of the "metafictional urge" that will develop fully in Albahari's later works. The setting of most stories is Zemun, a suburb of Belgrade, which once used to be a separate town in the Hapsburg Empire while Belgrade itself was under Ottoman rule. The Danube, the dividing point between these two civilizations within a single culture, is the great river along which family members take strolls and converse. This is a world of characters attempting to come to terms with their Jewish heritage, which always somehow escapes them. The stories question identity, which remains suspended, while memories flash through a stark narrative space. Father often cries; Mother has an uncanny ability to communicate with things.

The second and third parts of this selection explore the unfolding of language, which tells the story of its own becoming. This type of metafiction uses the short narrative form to probe the side of reality that is accessible only through language. On the other side are things, left in silence and surrounded by memories. "Do things know as much about us as we know about them?" asks the narrator in "Plastic Combs" (177). This question seems to be at the bottom of Albahari's efforts to come to terms with a reality whose fluidity often escapes the comprehension of his narrators. Reality is formulated as a question, riveted by constant interrogation of its conditions and limits, never slipping into a definite sense of "reality" that reaches beyond words. This "linguistic realism," already explored by Kiš in prose and Vasko Popa in poetry, approaches things with an almost amorous, fetishistic quality. Its probing into the realm of language-as-the-other-that-defines-me hovers between paranoia and narcissism, both predicated on the power of words to evoke things and their silent existence.

The insecurity and doubt of Albahari's narrators is encapsulated in the irony of the next sentence from "Plastic Combs": "I observed the hat but it did not respond" (177). If the first sentence poses a serious philosophical problem, the second one turns the problem into an epistemological parody. Albahari is wary of dispensing "truths" that extend beyond the immediate linguistic environment of his narrators, since they are painfully aware that the knowledge of things is inevitably tied to the words used to talk about them. Albahari's narrative universe is constantly imploding and shrinking, leaving the characters in a state of endless search for absurd clues that lead them nowhere. "Before he became what he is now, he contemplated writing a story about a writer who writes a story about a writer who no longer knows who, what, or where he is" (174). Albahari's prose articulates this absence of stable and knowable identity, a failure of identification that leaves traces and fragments of language in its wake.

The universe constructed by such a prose is inhabited by words and things that testify to the failure of language as representation. When "the author" tells "the boy" that "making one's way through metaphors is the only form of reality available to the two of them" (108), he is articulating Albahari's poetics of prose. Language functions as literature only as a constant return to its own rules of poetics, which often collide with "reality" based on consensus and mutual understanding. Relationships between humans are bound by a proliferating network of metaphors, which meander like labyrinths and create linguistic realities that are often opaque and unintelligible to the participants in a dialogue.

This is especially true for the second part of this selection, which is devoted mostly to dialogues between the narrator and his wife. Most of these humorous conversations are about literature and its conventions, with the wife playing devil's advocate. She undermines all the assumptions the narrator sets out to make about the nature of the literary process. These dialogues take place in a desolate, vacuous setting, which enhances the emotional wasteland each of the characters faces. There is a lot of intentional banality in these pieces, a narrative strategy that only enhances the humorous effect of Albahari's prose. This understated, almost demonic humor is perhaps Albahari's most valuable contribution to the Central European literary heritage.

. . .

As I have been writing these lines that concern a dear friend and one of my literary mentors, I have been experiencing real difficulty "ending" and "concluding" something about Albahari's literary opus. But then I realized that this kind of prose poses the ultimate challenge to the literary scholar. How does one end writing about a writer who always writes beyond ending? The reality beyond "reality" that Albahari's prose circumscribes is by definition inconclusive, uncertain, erratic. His prose testifies to that dimension that exceeds words, that remains hidden in the "halftones of unwritten music" he invokes in his story "The Playground." So, I end without ending, letting that music of words point toward that "something else" buried in the stories we tell each other.

▪ □ ▪ □ ▪

WRITINGS FROM AN UNBOUND EUROPE

Words Are Something Else
DAVID ALBAHARI

The Victory
HENRYK GRYNBERG

The Tango Player
CHRISTOPH HEIN

Balkan Blues: Writing Out of Yugoslavia
JOANNA LABON, ED.

Compulsory Happiness
NORMAN MANEA

Zenobia
GELLU NAUM

The Houses of Belgrade
The Time of Miracles
BORISLAV PEKIĆ

The Soul of a Patriot
EVGENY POPOV

Estonian Short Stories
KAJAR PRUUL AND DARLENE REDDAWAY, EDS.

Death and the Dervish
MEŠA SELIMOVIĆ

Fording the Stream of Consciousness
In the Jaws of Life and Other Stories
DUBRAVKA UGREŠIĆ

Ballad of Descent
MARTIN VOPĚNKA